SILVER LINING

A Romantic Suspense Novel

Aleatha Romig

New York Times, Wall Street Journal, and USA Today
bestselling author

COPYRIGHT AND LICENSE INFORMATION

SILVER LINING

A Romantic Suspense Novel

This is a work of fiction. Names, characters, places, and

incidents either are the product of the author's imagination or are used fictitiously, and any resemblance to any actual persons, living or dead, events, or locales is entirely coincidental.

2022 Edition License

SILVER LINING

"Your task is not to seek love, but merely to seek and find all barriers within yourself that you have built against it." ~ **Rumi**

When a wealthy powerful woman's life is threatened, she agrees to one week at a resort. What she doesn't expect is to meet a swoon worthy younger man capable of crumbling the walls around her heart. What happens when real life finds them face to face?

"A twisted, mysterious, romantic, steamy story that will grab you and keep you flipping pages."

From New York Times bestselling author Aleatha Romig comes a brand-new age-gap, forbidden romance, contemporary romantic-suspense novel in the world of high finance, where rules become blurred.

*SILVER LINING is a full-length, stand-alone novel.

Chapter One

Lena

Present time

The head of my security, Adam, gave me a nod as I touched the keycard to the sensor and a green light appeared. My bracelets jingled as I turned the knob, opening the door. Cool air met us as Adam stepped in front of me. The routine was part of our lives. My life. My temples pounded as he made a complete trek through the multiroom suite. After another nod and good night, Adam stepped out of the suite.

The door closed, the lock clicking. After securing the small chain, I closed my eyes, leaned against the solid barrier, and inhaled. The scent of eucalyptus filled my senses, replacing the aroma of the perfume I'd applied nearly ten hours ago.

Eucalyptus soothed me.

My therapist recommended a constant, something that made me feel secure even when I was away. The oil was my travel companion.

Kicking off my shoes, I sighed at the comfort from the lack of high heels and wiggled my toes against the cool gray tile. Step by step, I made my way through the eerily silent suite.

In the large living room area, the only illumination came from the city lights beyond the large panes. The pristine white furniture differed little from the white walls and long light-gray drapes.

The lights of New York City glistened with all the energy of the city itself. From this height in an upscale hotel, it was easy to forget the stench from piles of garbage accumulating on the sidewalk in the summer heat. Experience told me that the trash would be gone in the morning, only to return with the setting sun.

Removing my phone from my purse, I looked at the slew of emails. Opening one from my associate, I shook my head. The email was from Jeremy Wilde, my most trusted associate, letting me know the previous owners of Architech had contacted him again, asking about our decision on which employees would be retained from our recent acquisition. None, I wanted to reply. Two hundred and twenty million should silence them. Besides, I didn't have time to go through all the bios that my staff had compiled.

"You're hangry," I said to myself before I replied with a text message.

"Busy day today. Architech is a f'n gold mine. Can't you decide which ones to keep?"

He texted immediately back.

"Are you okay? Good day then? And no. I got the deal. I met employees. You will choose without bias."

His argument made sense. I could look at the bios objectively. Ignoring his first question, I replied.

I'll have a list of names by the time I'm back to Missoula tomorrow."

"As far as the day...if we're talking zeros, I have a good feeling." Before I hit send, I added, *"Tell the guys from Architech to go enjoy their windfall and stop pushing about the employees."*

"We promised," Jeremy texted back.

"Your name should be Jiminy. It's like you're my conscience."

"Someone has to be."

Tossing my phone on the table and entering the

small kitchen, I turned on the lights and found my dinner, the one I'd ordered this morning. The one that arrived three hours ago and sat unsupervised. A quick lift of the silver dome revealed the solidified Alfredo sauce covering the rubbery chicken and cold fettuccine noodles.

There was always the microwave.

As I lifted the plate, the gelled sauce jiggled, reminding me of Jell-O.

I wasn't a fan of Jell-O or of cold pasta.

With a shake of my head, I replaced the lid and went to the minibar disguised behind the sleek façade of a cabinet. After removing two small bottles of Johnny Walker Red, I made my way to the bathroom. The bright light fixtures over the vanity filled the space with stark illumination. For only a moment, I looked at my reflection.

Squaring my shoulders, I lifted my chin.

During today's marathon meeting with representatives of a well-known art gallery, I was *the* Lena Montgomery, the one whom others read about. The gallery wanted what Jeremy had secured nearly a month ago—the technology perfected by Architech, now owned by Venus, a subsidiary of Montgomery Holdings, which applied the concept of virtual environments.

Thinking about Architech reminded me to make a list.

Pulling names from a hat was objective—right?

I first became a player in the financial world by investing in the vision of others. Architech was an incredible vision. Now that it was ours, we controlled who had access.

Today's meeting was with a gallery interested in utilizing the technology.

Mr. and Mrs. Mueller, the gallery owners, were older yet open to the progressive endeavor of taking the gallery from within the confines of their brick-and-mortar building in the heart of their SoHo neighborhood to virtually anywhere and everywhere.

The people at the table with me today didn't know that their gallery had been what piqued my interest in Architech. They had been in negotiations with Architech directly until Venus stepped in.

The price had gone up.

They were outbid.

Now I had the reins, and the gallery was courting me to license what was now mine.

Opening my eyes wide, I took in the light shade of brown in the reflection. Those eyes met every gaze in the room today. My questions as well as my answers were quick and as they say, on the money. Everyone in that room knew that I held the power to make their dream a reality. They also understood that I could walk away.

That precipice was where I wanted to leave them.

I could have returned to the hotel in time for my dinner to be warm, but I didn't.

Taking a deep breath, I let the corners of my lips move upward and my cheeks lift.

At six o'clock, the gallery was a bit too cocky for my liking. I wasn't ready to end the day on that note. When we said our final good nights at nearly nine o'clock, the ball was back in my court. Tomorrow, they'd be willing to pay what I proposed, or I'd leave. They weren't the only interested partners.

Unscrewing the cap on the Johnny Walker, I lifted the bottle to my lips, leaving a red ring around the mouth of the bottle from what remained of my lipstick, and swallowed. The amber liquid burned as it coated my tongue and throat. Slamming the empty bottle on the vanity, I felt my smile grow as the sound echoed through the large suite.

I mentally made a list of things to do before tomorrow morning.

Emails.

Go over the gallery's updated proposal.

Never could I have imagined this life as a young girl.

It was busy, productive, and better than what I'd dreamed.

My life could be filled with warm dinners and a house full of people. I'd had the model. My father, mother, sister, and I had the picturesque home in suburban Chicago. Being the older daughter, I imagined going to college and settling down near my family. Marriage was an assumption. Of the two of us, my sister, Madison, was the quieter one, more of a dreamer. I was the take-charge one.

As her older sister, I had been told since she was brought home from the hospital that she was my responsibility.

That reality hit home when our parents were killed in an automobile accident. At a little older than twenty, my life changed in ways I never imagined—both of our lives did. My plans for a normal, quiet life slipped through my fingers. Our new reality took Madison and me on a bumpy ride.

I'd like to say we both were better for it, but that wouldn't be true.

My sister moved to Texas after I lost everything that was supposed to keep us stable. That wasn't completely accurate. I trusted the wrong person, a person who stole our inheritance and tried to take my dignity too.

My gaze narrowed as I studied my own face—my cheekbones, my nose, my lips. When a person hit bottom, they had a choice. Over twenty years ago, I pulled myself off the floor and made the decision that my dignity wasn't up for sale. I would succeed in life, and I would do so with no regrets.

I wasn't a dreamer. I was a doer.

The truth was that when I first began this quest, I was miserably ill-prepared to take on the financial giants who I now call by their first names. Thankfully, I was and am a fast learner. I surrounded myself with like-minded people. Those of us who made a name for ourselves—by ourselves—were a rare breed. We weren't raised with a silver spoon or surrounded by the glitz and glamor of mansions or even the executive suite at The Langham on Fifth Avenue.

No, we hide the metaphoric dirt of our past with expensive manicures and the bruises with designer-named apparel. That didn't mean that we didn't remember when those same fingers were bloodied, nails broken, and bruises visible.

We remembered because if we forgot about our climb and our clawing our way to the top, we could become comfortable.

Comfort was a luxury.

Comfort would be living on investments and forgoing the marathon negotiations.

Comfort was earned.

My attention went to the inviting large clawfoot tub. The emails could wait. I'd earned a bath.

Chapter Two

Lena

The tub's porcelain was smooth and cool beneath my touch. Turning on the glistening faucet, I waited until the water reached the warmth I wanted and added eucalyptus oil to the swirling water. As I poured the second bottle of Johnny into a crystal tumbler, I found my cellphone and made a call to the man in the suite across the hallway.

"Ms. Montgomery," Adam answered on the second ring.

"Adam, I'm sure you're settled in and for that, I'm sorry."

"Not settled. What can I do for you?"

"My dinner is cold. I know I said we were done for the night, but if all I have for dinner is what I can find in the minibar, my head will be throbbing during tomorrow's eight a.m. meeting."

Adam scoffed.

I imagined his smile, the way it quirked up on one side and the light blue of his eyes.

There was nothing remotely sexual between Adam and me. He was an employee—mine. He worked for me and had for over seven years. I trusted him with my life.

It was my heart that I kept locked away—from everyone.

That childhood assumption of marriage disappeared the night I was beaten black and blue because stealing my sister's and my inheritance wasn't enough for that man. That night, I was prepared to end Logan Butler's life. Thankfully, a friend, Donovan Sherman, came to my aid, convincing me that there was better revenge than any that would result in incarceration.

That was when I swore off the idea of a home with a white picket fence.

Over my forty-three years, I'd had my share of one-night stands, longer relationships, and friends with benefits. I'd found and given pleasure in the company of both men and women, rarely at the same time, but I couldn't say never.

My mind went to CJ, the man I'd recently met,

reminding me of our one week in paradise. Two ships passing in the night—as the story goes. Yet during our one week, I felt the walls I'd built around my heart, those I thought to be indestructible, begin to crack. We agreed to walk away with no regrets.

I could rebuild.

"Ms. Montgomery."

Shaking my head, my thoughts returned to Adam. Yes, my bodyguard was attractive, but sleeping with an employee was my hard line—forbidden by my own rule. It was difficult enough to be taken seriously in this world as a woman. I refused to be a notch on someone's belt, someone who worked for me.

Adam spoke again, "I'd be happy to get you something to eat. I saw that the shop on the first floor had salads. If I hurry, they should still be open."

The energy from today's meeting and the whiskey coursing through my veins combined to rekindle a memory of a late night next to a small private pool. The sky above was peppered with stars, and the warm air grew sultrier by the minute. CJ's turquoise stare was set on mine as he fed me from the box he'd procured.

With a grin, I said, "Pizza. Thin crust, big slice—the kind you have to fold. New York pizza."

"Shouldn't you be a Chicago pizza woman?"

I dusted the dirt from Chicago off me a long time ago—the city where my parents died, where I last recalled my sister happy, and where I hit bottom. It was also the city where I began my climb.

"I think you know me better than that," I said. "I prefer almost anywhere to Chicago."

"Pizza it is."

"Thank you, Adam. I'm going to take a bath. Please leave the food in the kitchen, soggy container and all. Oh, and extra napkins."

"Did you lock the chain lock?"

My gaze fluttered toward the hallway and to the door beyond my suite. "I'll undo the chain." Before he could answer, I added, "And you have a key."

"I'll be back as soon as I can. I have a camera set and an alarm if your door opens. I can see all that information from my phone. Hotel security is also working with me."

"Thank you. I know you have everything covered." As I disconnected the call, a shiver ran through me, leaving a trail of goose bumps. Adam was the only security detail I'd brought along on this current trip. I could have brought more or hired more in the city. I also had female members of my security who could stay in the suite with me. One, Kelsey, was currently staying in my home. This was a short trip, and I preferred my privacy.

Up until this moment, I hadn't given the one-man team much thought. My mind had been consumed with computer graphics and virtual environments, and the potential that they held.

Brushing off the uneasy feeling, I walked down the tiled hallway, unlocked the chain, and peered through the peephole. Within the distorted view I saw the back of Adam's head and his broad shoulders. The suit coat he'd worn all day was gone. When he turned, I noticed his tie too was gone and his collar opened. After securing the door to his suite, my bodyguard disappeared in search of delicious, greasy pizza.

"Stop being paranoid," I told myself as the scent of eucalyptus reminded me of my filling clawfoot tub. Closing the blinds to the city forty stories below, I turned on every light in the suite.

It wasn't paranoia if someone was actually out to get you.

Once back in the bathroom, with humidity hanging in the air and coating the large mirrors, I peeled off my blouse and skirt, tossing them onto the floor along with my panties and bra. The water rose as

I stepped into the water. My skin quickly pinkened at the warmth. The ends of my auburn hair dampened as I laid my head back against the raised end of the tub. With the oil coating my skin, I inhaled the soothing aroma as the water's warmth and a drink from my tumbler chased away the earlier chill.

It wasn't unusual for a person with my wealth and high-profile life to employ security. While I kicked ass in the world of finance, my self-defense skills were limited. I'd been coached and had practiced over the years. In a gym with an instructor, I knew what to do. Nevertheless, I was a five-foot, six-inch woman weighing a hundred and thirty pounds—according to my driver's license. Reality was an extra ten pounds.

Even so, having Adam or another of my security with me had become natural.

And then, about three months ago, it became a necessity.

First there were unexplainable coincidences. I blew them off as nerves or stress. There were always fires and deadlines.

And then the break-in.

I traveled too much to have a pet.

In reality, I was probably too selfish for a pet, but that was a truth I had yet to explore with my therapist.

I found a happy medium. The tropical fish tank in my home reminded me of the blue waters of the Caribbean, while snowcapped mountains glistened under the Montana blue sky, the place I currently called home.

I'd grown fond of the aquarium and its inhabitants. I'd even named the clown fish. No, it wasn't Nemo. His name was Bozo, after a clown on television in Chicago during my childhood.

One day when I arrived home from a business trip, the front door of my home was ajar.

Even in the warm tub, the memory made my skin clammy.

Adam entered the house first. Once it was determined that there was no immediate threat, he led me inside. We walked in silence from room to room as the feeling I'd had years ago came back to me.

Violated.

This time it wasn't my body, and yet it felt just as personal.

The power had been turned off, rendering my security system and cameras useless. My home office had been ransacked, computers stolen, and screens smashed.

The large tank that separated my office from the living room had been electrocuted, essentially frying my beloved fish, including Bozo. The potent stench lingered in the house long after the tank was restored.

The new fish didn't have names.

Whomever the intruder was, he or she hadn't given up the torment.

Every now and again, a fish was delivered in the mail or left on my doorstep. Sometimes to my home and other times to my office. The fish were always tropical and always dead. Adam and his team made improvements—added cameras and alarms.

Three weeks ago, I received a box of candy with a handwritten note. The chocolate pieces had been injected with cyanide. Following the urging of the police and my associates, I left the country for one week. It gave the investigators time to work and me, distance.

Despite the luxury of my warm bath, I rarely took time for myself. The fact that I was smiling at the memories meant it was a good week. When I returned home, I hit the ground running. That was what brought me to New York.

Missoula was a beautiful city where nature was always near. No longer did I run or bike alone. I hated every minute of feeling smothered. And yet I refused to stop living because someone had me in their sights.

The reality was that while I'd clawed my way to the top, I'd made friends and enemies.

The current theory was that someone wanted revenge.

I knew the feeling.

It was being on this side that was new.

Chapter Three

Chandler

Three weeks ago

Out on the balcony, I lifted my face toward the blue sky and closed my eyes. The sounds of the ocean filled my ears as the salty breeze brushed my skin. And yet I couldn't enjoy it; my thoughts were too consumed.

Concentrate on the positive.

That was what my father would say.

Opening my eyes, I took one more step toward the railing. The metal, warmed by the sun, singed my palm, and still, I gripped the edge and looked down. Twenty stories below was a crystal blue pool that wound around the beachfront, complete with palm trees and umbrellas. Some of the loungers were along the pool's edge while others were partially submerged.

"Multimillionaire plunges to his death at five-star Caribbean resort."

The thought made me smile.

It wasn't that I wanted to jump, but the thought was there.

"Positive, CJ," I said to the breeze.

My bank account contained more money than I'd ever imagined.

Hell, at only thirty-one years of age, I could retire. I'd need to invest well, but it would be possible. I could go back to Ohio and live a life like my parents—walks in the park, swimming at the city pool, Tuesday night dinners at the Moose, and summers spent watching the Reds.

I could be like the commercial said and become my parents.

My grip of the railing tightened.

Becoming the people who raised my brother and me was never the goal for either of us. They were good, hardworking people who loved their simple existence. The path Colton and I took wasn't to become wealthy. It was to do more than our father and grandfather. Never in our wildest dreams did we think that we'd become a major or even minor player in the world of virtual reality.

We started with a concept to improve gaming.

With my degree in computer and information technology and Colton's in numerical analysis, we had the basic concepts covered. Together, we founded Architech, spending nights and weekends until we found what we liked, what we couldn't find anywhere else. It was the entire experience of virtual gaming, utilizing all the senses. We imagined pitching the idea to one of the top gaming companies and sent out a few feelers.

The long and the short of it was that our technology was sought after by an even larger market. Hotels, art galleries, and museums were only a few of the interested parties. The next year was spent securing our patent. The expenses increased exponentially, yet we weren't ready to give up. We rented space and began manufacturing. With time the number of employees grew.

My life was filled with development, production, distribution...the list went on and on.

And now it's all gone.

A week ago, Colton and I signed away our baby, what we'd put our hearts and souls into at the expense of what many considered a normal life. Venus Holdings came out of nowhere with an offer that we couldn't refuse. The representative we dealt with was a man named Jeremy Wilde. It wasn't only the money that made the deal special. Venus offered to retain some of our employees.

More money and securing our employees' future—at least for a little while—was a compromise we were both willing to make. Our employees were people who took a chance on two young men thinking outside the box. Selling Architech should benefit them as well as us.

The vibration of my phone pulled me from my thoughts. My brother's name was on the screen. "Colt," I said, after a swipe of the green icon.

"Living the life?"

I scoffed as I looked out to the horizon. "I'm bored out of my fucking mind."

"How long have you been in Cancún?"

"An hour or so."

Colton laughed. "You're not bored. You haven't started to enjoy yourself."

"What if Venus fucks it all up?" I didn't need to explain 'it.' My brother and I'd had this conversation a thousand different ways.

"They won't. Jeremy said that Venus has the assets to get the software and hardware to a global level. Man, we both agreed. That's why I called. The third install-ment just hit our account. While you're gone, I'll do the math and figure out the severance packages for anyone who Venus doesn't retain."

More money.

Why didn't this make me happy?

Cool air hit me as I entered the bedroom of my suite and pulled the glass door closed behind me. I ran my free hand over my chin-length hair, realizing I hadn't tethered it back this morning before catching my flight. My chin and cheeks were stubbly. In all honesty, I barely made it to the gate in time. My heart wasn't in this getaway.

It was back with Architech—the company that no longer was ours.

"I'm going to give him a call," I said.

"Jeremy? Why? The deal is done."

With the final payment, we had seventy-two hours to change our mind. "It is, but if Venus is willing to keep some employees, I want to be one of them."

"You what? You want to be an employee of the company you owned?"

"No, I want to work for Venus and stay in control of the company we built from the ground up." Looking around at the expensive furnishing of this posh resort, I added, "I'm too young to be traveling the world. I'm feeling fucking useless without something to do. Pokémon can't fill my days and nights." That was more of a dig at Colt. I played, but not like he and his wife did. Going out to dinner with them was constantly a search for gyms, characters, or battles.

"Do something else, CJ," Colton said. "Haven't you heard, nine-to-five jobs were invented for boomers? Hell, you've always been good at investing. Spend your days researching the markets and day trade. Or better yet, go down to the pool and meet a girl."

A girl.

Colton was married. That wasn't for me. My new goal was to stay with our technology and make sure it didn't get fucked up. The mattress bounced as I flopped onto the large bed and stared up at the ceiling. "I'm an asset to Venus. No one knows our work better than the two of us."

"Spend the week relaxing. You remember how to do that, right?"

"I should have brought someone along. Going from working twenty-four seven to having nothing but free time is making my skin crawl."

"Devon and I would have joined you."

A smile curls my lips. "That would be great. I love being the third wheel." I had nothing against Devon, my sister-in-law. I liked that she and Colton have been together since college, when our start-up was just a passion.

Yeah, having money meant I'd never know if a woman liked me or my bank account. I sure fucked up on finding someone early on like Colton did. Ripe old age of thirty-one.

"Stop acting like a loser," he said. "You're young, in great shape, and have unlimited funds. Spend this week soaking up the sun and meeting some ladies. Next week you can call Jeremy if you still want to become employed by Venus."

"Are you skimming some of the third installment? What's with all these compliments?"

"You basically quit living or doing anything besides Architech since your junior year at OSU. I had a few more years before we both were buried in work. And yeah, I have Devon. I love what you and I accomplished. I also feel guilty. Go find a life even if it's only for a week."

Turning my head toward the glass doors, I realized my older brother might be right. I could do this. I could learn to relax for one week, and after that, it would be back to work. "Okay, I'm hanging up before you start singing or some shit."

Colton laughed. "That will be you at the pool bar."

"Fine. Give Devon my love."

"Text now and then, CJ. Mom's worried about you being alone in Mexico. She's sure you're in mortal danger."

"This place is secure. It's one of their taglines. That means it's true, right?"

"Sounds legit."

"Bye."

After disconnecting the call, I stood and walked back onto the balcony. Looking back down at the pool, I spotted multiple empty lounges.

"You're in Cancún at one of the best resorts," I mumbled to myself. "Stop whining about selling the company and maybe after a week, things will look different." I wasn't certain if I was continuing Colton's pep talk, or if I was trying to convince myself. Either way, I pulled my t-shirt over my head and dropped trou. Stepping out of my shorts and kicking my canvas loafers to the side, I searched for my suitcase.

"Well, shit."

I realized it was still in the living area. Completely nude, I went on a search for my bag.

"Oh," a woman in a hotel uniform said as her eyes widened and she spun away. "I'm sorry, sir."

"Shit," I stuttered. "I didn't hear you."

"I'm filling your refrigerator." She turned back

with pink in her cheeks and her eyes everywhere but on me, well, all of me. "I'll go."

A laugh bubbled up from my throat like I couldn't recall laughing in too long. "I'm grabbing my suitcase. Finish what you need to do. No sense leaving now."

"Sí."

Shaking my head, I made my way with my suitcase back into the bedroom and soon had on my swimming trunks and sandals. I'd thrown a few things together at the last minute before leaving my apartment. I'd need to buy some sunscreen in one of the shops.

Placing a baseball cap on my head, I grabbed a two-hundred pesos bill from my wallet, before tossing my wallet into a bag with my towel. On my way out, I laid the two hundred on the counter near the woman. When she turned my way, my smile grew. "This is for you. Sorry for the show."

"Oh no, señor. This is my job."

"Please."

She bashfully looked my way as she reached for the cash. "I'll make more noise next time."

Leaving the room, I couldn't help but wonder if parading around naked would be the highlight of my vacation or if it was only the start.

Colt wanted me to relax.

Sun and a cool drink were next on my agenda.

Chapter Four

Lena

Three weeks ago

My wide-brimmed hat shaded my face, and my dark sunglasses covered my tired eyes. Escaping to a Mexican resort wasn't something I normally did, especially not all alone. In reality, I wasn't alone. My security detail was nearby. This trip I had two bodyguards along with me. The resort where Gigi, my assistant, had booked a week's stay was one of the best along the coast. Secluded with all the amenities that an all-inclusive resort had to offer, including its boast of safety.

That was the point of this getaway, to get away, incognito, and try to relax.

There were too many balls currently in the air both

personally and professionally. After the recent security issues, I was convinced to fly below the radar. And after completing a recent acquisition, I agreed to lie low—if only for a short reprieve.

The e-reader in my hand had gone dark.

Concentrating on anything was currently out of my wheelhouse. It was difficult to submerse myself in fiction when reality was like a marathon of *The Twilight Zone*. Closing my eyes, I rested my head back against the chair and took a mental inventory.

Jeremy, my assistant turned business partner sent me a text to let me know that the final installment had been made to Architech, the company Venus Holdings acquired.

That meant in three days the deal would be done. There was no turning back on the sellers' part. I felt my smile as I thought about the possibilities for this relatively new technology. Truly, I'd gotten Architech for less than I anticipated. It was Jeremy's idea to offer the retention of some of the employees for a trial period. Since I didn't attend any of the meetings, I trusted Jeremy's gut. He'd met, face-to-face, the founders of Architech—two brothers with the surname of Thompson—and claimed they were stand-up guys who cared about their employees.

I could play nice for a while. However, once the

agreed-upon period was over, I'd clean house. The three-month trial would give us time to learn who was valuable and who was expendable. My concern wasn't about the employees as much as it was on licensing the technology. As soon as it was public that Venus had acquired Architech for two hundred and twenty million, the offers started to come in. In the current environment, we'd recoup our expenditure in less than a year. And then the sky was the limit.

Yes, in the chaos that was my life, the deal was good.

There was also the matter of my sister, Madison. Without going into detail, she was in the custody of the state of Wisconsin in a maximum-security institution. My sister wasn't a monster. She was misguided, misunderstood, and currently undergoing psychiatric care.

She was also guilty of a crime.

I knew that without a doubt because the man she shot was my good friend. It was all rather complicated. Currently, I was sparing no expense on her care. My legal team was working on a plea bargain. If the state of Wisconsin agreed to reduce the charge to a class F felony, she will plead guilty. The sentence could be a fine of $25,000, a prison sentence of twelve and a half years, or both.

There wasn't a right answer to this. Yet no matter

what, Madison was my sister, and I would help in ways I should have been doing before. Just thinking about how much she's lost made my heart and soul hurt.

Maybe it was because of Madison that I took this time away. I'd been so focused on my companies and success, on climbing the ladder, that I'd neglected people, people like my sister. There was also my friend Donovan who was injured—he was doing much better. Not only had he recovered from the injury, but he married a woman he definitely didn't deserve.

Van and I go way back. We were jokingly supposed to end up together if we both remained single. The thought made me smirk. While we'd enjoyed one another's company in a sexual way, the two of us together were better in the boardroom than the bedroom. He made the right decision when he proposed to his now wife.

I was happy for them both.

Van and I were like-minded in our pursuit of success. If he could let someone into the walls he'd built and take time to smell the roses, maybe I could too. Not that I was looking for anyone to let into my walls—no, I'd put them up brick by brick. Opening my eyes and seeing the sun glistening on the sea like diamonds, I hoped that perhaps I could take a week to enjoy a bit of the bounty I'd accumulated and drift away from the daily pressures.

"Ma'am."

Looking up I saw Kelsey, one half of my current security team. She didn't look like a bodyguard in her flowing beach cover and sunglasses. That was the point. She was blending in. "Yes?"

"Adam is over there." She tilted her head. "I'm heading upstairs for a little while; this sun is brutal on my eyes. I wanted you to know you're not alone."

A grin came to my lips as I scanned the resort's pool area. I was not alone. That was for sure. The chairs were filling quickly with people, those like me wanting to enjoy the sun and surf and possibly a few too many drinks with tiny umbrellas. "Thank you, Kelsey."

"Will you dine in one of the restaurants tonight?"

My bathing-suit-clad breasts pushed forward as I inhaled. "I haven't decided."

It was her turn to smile. "It looks good on you."

I peered down at my bathing suit. Keeping myself in shape was something I enjoyed. Parading in front of strangers in a two-piece bathing suit, not so much. The fact they were strangers and no one knew my name made it easier. "The suit?"

"No, I mean, yes. What I meant was seeing you relax. It's a rarity. You deserve it."

"Then why do I feel like a kid skipping school?"

Kelsey tilted her head toward the mostly melted daiquiri at my side. "Maybe you need another."

"Maybe."

"See, you're doing it. Going with the flow. Not being planned and regimented."

She was right. My usual life was planned daily to the minute. From waking to laying my head down at night, every moment was accounted for.

"Are you saying I'm boring—usually?" I asked with a grin.

"No. Usually, you're a force to be reckoned with and that's admirable. It's just nice to see you letting your guard down. It's good for you to not think about things for a while. Adam and I have your back."

"Thank you, Kelsey."

As she walked away, I waved down a young man in a resort shirt and shorts and ordered a fresh daiquiri. Time slipped away as I laid the chair back and closed my eyes. The sounds around me faded as the rum circulated through my veins and my mind drifted.

Gasping, I woke with a start. Shaking my head, I looked around, wondering what had startled me. Everything was as it had been. Adam was still sitting at a small table. When our eyes met, his opened wide. I shook my head, letting him know I was all right.

I was all right.

If I said it enough, maybe I'd believe it as well.

Whatever woke me wasn't real. It was a dream. The details were out of reach as they'd been since the break-in...

I took a deep breath

More chairs were filled than before my nap. Needing to stretch my legs, I sat up, slipped my feet into my sandals, and walked to the closest bar. With one empty stool, I leaned in between two people to place an order.

The man on my right turned my way.

I'd be lying if I said I hadn't been checking him out as I approached. His wide shoulders, muscular arms, and trim waist did more than catch my attention. I was instantly intrigued with his tattoos. However, it was as he turned that I had to stop myself from verbally reacting. He was incredibly handsome with turquoise eyes similar to the color of the ocean's water, and longer dark hair tethered into a short ponytail at the nape of his neck. His chin and cheeks were covered with the right amount of stubble.

"Hi," he said in a deep timbre with a sexy grin.

Thank goodness I was wearing my sunglasses. Hopefully, they hid my ogling. "Hi."

"May I help you?" the bartender asked. She was a cute blond in short shorts and a tank top.

"Yes, I wondered if I could see a menu." By my overreaction to this man, it was clear that the two daiquiris I'd consumed meant that I was in need of food.

The bartender nodded toward the stool. "You can have a seat."

"That's a good idea," Mr. Handsome said.

Warmth filled my cheeks.

When was the last time I blushed?

That wasn't me.

Yes, food. I needed food.

Looking back to the bartender, I replied, "No. I already have a chair over there." I pointed. "Could someone bring it out to me?"

"Yes, of course."

As I turned to walk away, Mr. Handsome spoke, "I don't bite."

I spun back toward him.

His grin grew. "Unless it's something you like."

It was difficult to gauge someone's age when they were wearing orange swim trunks and no shirt. Nevertheless, I was pretty certain that I was the older of the two. With maturity came wisdom and experience. "Oh, I prefer to be the aggressor, not the prey."

He turned my direction on the stool, giving me a full-on view of his tight abs. "Sounds like a challenge."

"No, simply a statement." I nodded with a smile. "Enjoy the sun."

With each step away, my pulse thumped in my ears. I felt his stare on me—or maybe I wanted it to be true. When I reached my chair, I turned back to the bar and grinned. His stunning gaze was still on me as I sat. Lifting his drink in the air, he mouthed "cheers."

With my empty glass, I returned the gesture.

"Your menu, señora."

Chapter Five

Chandler / CJ

The treadmill faced the window, giving me a panoramic view as the sun rose slowly, creeping up from the horizon. There had been only one other person in the resort gym when I entered. Gauging by the music and voices that I'd heard from my balcony going on into the early morning hours, many of the guests were now still blissfully asleep.

As the pitch of the treadmill climbed, I concentrated on my footing.

Right. Left. Right.

Pumping my arms, I neared the crest of the imagery hill.

Higher and higher.

My shins tightened as I pushed harder and faster.

This I could do. I could push myself, punish myself to the brink.

It would ultimately give me a small bit of satisfaction.

Yesterday was a bust.

Whether for relaxing or moving on, being closer to the equator didn't accomplish either.

After a few hours at the pool bar, I retired to my suite, ordered room service, and sat alone on the balcony with my dinner and a bottle of Blanton's.

Maybe I had forgotten what it was like to have fun.

Back in the gym, sweat dripped from my brow and from my pulled-back hair. The stench of day-old whiskey emanated from my perspiration. There was a likely possibility that I'd had more than my share last night.

The only thought that pulled me away from my wallowing about Architech was that of the woman at the pool bar yesterday afternoon. Damn, her seductive smile infiltrated my thoughts. As if she were truly present, as the night progressed, her image became clearer—her dark auburn hair shone under the star-filled sky. The way her bathing suit covered enough of her sexy curves to make me wonder what was beneath was imprinted in my mind. I heard her breathy tone, "Oh, I prefer to be the aggressor, not the prey."

During the afternoon, one hundred times or more, I contemplated going over to her lounge chair and speaking to her.

Once she was fully seated, my view was only of her toned legs, bronzing in the sunshine. By the time I had my courage up, or maybe my alcohol level, she was gone.

What the fuck was I going to do, wow her with my big cash-out?

It was hard to wow someone with something you regretted.

The treadmill to my far left now had a jogger.

As the sky lightened, I turned to my left.

The woman was probably my age. There was no way those tits were real.

Her lips turned upward when she caught me looking her way.

With a bit of a grin, I turned away, becoming engrossed in the dawn of the morning sky before me. With her light-colored hair and bouncing boobs, she could be exactly what Colton meant for me to find. The thing was, I didn't want to find a woman like that. The only thing she lacked was a neon sign saying she was ready and willing for a vacation tryst.

Wasn't that what Colton meant?

As the gym filled with more people, I began to think about taking my run out onto the beach. It was as I started my cooldown that the treadmill between bouncy-boob lady and me came to life. The slender fingers pushed the buttons like a professional. My breath caught as I turned.

Her big hat was gone, but in a second, I knew she was the woman from the bar.

Wiping my forehead and neck with the towel, I smiled her direction.

"It's you," she said.

Without her sunglasses, I could see the soft shade of brown in her eyes. Her hair was curled in ringlets. She was wearing a sports bra and stretch shorts, enough to cover her, but little enough to show the tone of her body. Toned with the perfect amount of softness.

A grin spread across my lips. "The predator, right?"

Her gaze glistened. "When necessary."

"You know, the thing about predators, or you said *aggressor* yesterday...there is always a greater predator. The bear is king in the west, but take that same bear to the safari and" —I shake my head— "he's up against tigers and lions."

She began walking briskly before turning my way. "You do realize the lioness is the hunter."

"My name is CJ." I offered her my hand.

"I don't recall asking."

Taking my hand back, I smirked at her spirit. The lioness was playing with her next meal.

"Touché. You didn't ask. I offered."

She continued to look straight ahead, but I could see her uplifted cheeks and grin in the reflection of the glass.

I went on, "I offered because you are the lioness. I prefer to stay on the good side of predators such as yourself."

"And you, CJ, are you a predator or prey?"

"Lately, I'd say predator." I took a breath. "Though to be honest, I'm not too thrilled about it."

Just as her walking began to speed up, she turned to me with a smile. "Lena."

As my cooldown slowed, a quick look behind me let me know there were people waiting for my machine. Another wipe of my face and neck. "Lena, would you like to join me for breakfast by the infinity pool?"

Her eyes opened wide before she grinned. "CJ, I think it's better if I say no."

Ignoring the people behind us, I nodded. "I respect

that. I disagree, but I respect it." I looked at my watch. It was only 6:15 a.m. "I'll be waiting at eight thirty, table for two, coffee and mimosas. The menu is filled with delicacies for carnivores and vegetarians alike." In actuality, I had no clue what was on the menu.

I shot her my best smile. "After all, even lionesses need to eat."

"Do you know who I am?" she asked.

"You're Lena. The woman from the bar who I've been thinking about since yesterday."

Pink filled her cheeks as her shoulders squared. "I'm not that simple."

Bowing at the waist, I nodded. "Good. I'm supposed to spend this week relaxing, and to be honest, it's boring as hell. I could really use some complication."

Her pert breasts pushed forward as she inhaled. Finally, she nodded. "Eight thirty. I'll ask the hostess for—"

"C.J." I grinned. "I'll be waiting for you, Lena."

With one last look back at her tight round ass in the stretchy shorts, I walked away. It wasn't until I got back up to my suite that I allowed myself to think about what I'd just done.

This was crazy. I should have spoken to the woman with the boobs, not that Lena didn't have boobs... It was that the other woman didn't attract me. Lena—oh hell yes.

Last night on the balcony and really, ever since I saw her yesterday, I'd been thinking about her. Now I knew her name. I'd seen her smile and heard her voice. The fantasies I'd concocted while under the influence of whiskey were sparking to life in my thoughts, small connections setting off explosions that had my entire body on edge.

In the bedroom, I kicked off my tennis shoes and socks, stripped away my sweaty t-shirt and shorts. Before dropping my boxers, I checked to be sure there wasn't anyone else in the suite. With the coast clear, my boxers joined the mix on the floor in need of laundering.

"You do realize the lioness is the hunter."

The memory of that response, combined with my not-so-PG fantasies, was recirculating my blood flow. With each step toward the bathroom, I grew harder.

The lights in the bathroom illuminated the glass and shiny fixtures. I caught a glimpse of myself in the large mirrors. Sweat glistened from my skin as pre-come shone at the end of my erection.

For the first time since I signed my name on the hundred dotted lines, I felt alive.

I imagined Lena completing her workout, her skin

shimmering with perspiration as she ran the treadmill's course. That workout morphed from the resort gym to the two of us—alone.

My fingers surrounded my cock that for the first time in forever was also alive. Veins showed upon the surface as they gorged with blood, and my balls tightened.

"Fuck," I growled as I moved my hand up and down.

Before the temperature of the shower could warm, I stepped under the cool spray, closing the glass door behind me. With one hand on the tile, I leaned forward. My breathing caught as I tightened my grip.

Behind my closed lids, I pictured the legs soaking up the sun now wrapped around me. My cock buried deep inside her as her walls contracted around me. Faster my hand moved as I held my breath. Her soft brown eyes were staring deep into my gaze as our bodies pounded and slapped against the other.

Shit, the end was close.

Explosions ignited behind my closed eyes as come painted the tile of the shower wall. String after string. Laying my head back, I let out a roar. The deep sound echoed against the glass and tile. Tilting my forehead toward the wall, I grinned. "You may be a lioness, Lena, but then I'm the lion. You hunt—for me."

The shower, having grown incrementally hotter, reddened my skin. With my face now toward the stream, I turned down the temperature of the water and let the cooler spray refresh and invigorate me.

Just maybe this wouldn't be a boring week.

Chapter Six

Lena

"You agreed?" Kelsey asked with a grin.

I shrugged, knowing that the heat in my cheeks gave me away. "It's only breakfast."

Kelsey smiled. "I'll run a background check. What's his name?"

"He said CJ, but I don't want a background check."

"Ms. Montgomery, I don't recommend—"

"We spoke yesterday at the pool," I said, interrupting her, "and I purposely chose the treadmill beside him."

Kelsey and I were alone in the elevator, the one taking us up to our suites on the top floor. Today's workout wasn't unusual. The two of us regularly spent our mornings in the gym. When in Missoula, that gym was in my home. When away, we continued the practice. I understood Kelsey's job was to protect me, but I also believed she enjoyed the physical exertion. With my normal routines, my security spent a great deal of time standing and overseeing. The time in the gym was our break from the usual employer-employee relationship. Her use of my surname meant she was in business mode.

"He's not a stalker," I continued, and after a deep breath clarified, "My fish/candy stalker." Not wanting to think about that, I added, "It could be said I was stalking him."

Kelsey's smile broadened only to fade. "A background check would be wise nonetheless."

"No," I replied definitively. "It's only breakfast, and I don't know his last name."

"That isn't a problem. He's staying here. Adam can access the reservations."

I contemplated Adam searching the resort's reservation list. "If CJ brings a dead fish to breakfast, fine. Otherwise, for now, I'd like to pretend to be a normal woman who learns about a man from that man, not from my security team."

"Normal," Kelsey scoffed.

"Remember," I replied as the elevator came to a stop, "you're the one who told me to relax."

We stepped from the elevator into the empty hallway. At this time of morning everything was still relatively quiet. Yet CJ was up and working out.

Kelsey spoke low as we passed closed doors. "I'd still feel better if we did a quick check."

"I'll decide after breakfast."

Together, we walked to the door of my suite. As I unlocked the door, Kelsey waited. After the door was opened, she nodded and walked past me, entering the suite. The increase in my pulse as I waited in silence thumped in my ears. I'd blame the onset of nervousness on the mental reminder of the dead fish. It wasn't until Kelsey returned and announced that everything was clear that I finally released my breath.

"Thank you."

"Breakfast by the infinity pool at eight thirty," she confirmed, recalling what I'd told her of CJ's invitation.

"Yes."

"Adam will escort you."

I turned, meeting Kelsey's stare, and straightened my five feet, six inches to its full height. "He will watch from afar." I wasn't asking.

The idea of being escorted by Adam to a breakfast with CJ didn't sit well with my ambition of being a normal woman. I imagined the conversation.

Who is that?

My bodyguard.

Who are you? Why do you have a bodyguard?

Yep, not happening.

"Remember what happened—"

I didn't let Kelsey finish. "My mind is made up. I believe you and Adam work for me."

"Yes, we do. It's our job to keep you safe." Kelsey took a deep breath. "Please keep your watch on."

"Of course."

My watch was a tracker. It wasn't some amazing spy technology. It was simply an Apple watch, the same as half the population wore. I thought about her comment a few minutes later as I unfastened the band and laid it on the vanity.

Once I'd rid myself of my damp workout clothes and drank a bottle of water, I stepped under the spray of the shower, washed away the perspiration from my workout, and began to think about what was to come.

Why did I agree to breakfast?

It was out of character.

There was something about CJ that made me want to be out of character.

Being completely honest with myself, I agreed to breakfast because I wanted to. I wanted CJ to come over to my lounge chair yesterday. That wasn't like me. I'd stopped waiting for men to make the first move a long time ago. And yet I wanted to see if he would.

Yesterday, as I ate my lunch, my thoughts continually went back to him, to his turquoise stare and his wide shoulders, the same shoulders and muscular back I noticed when I entered the gym. All afternoon I'd wanted to lean away from the shade over my lounge chair and see if he was still there or if he was talking to another woman or a man.

It was a bit of neediness I didn't recognize in myself.

Maybe it was basic, wanting to know that I was still a woman. That for a sliver of time, I wanted simple basics—a woman and a man. No knowledge of who I was, no knowledge of what I did. Just girl meets boy.

Well, if girl was forty-three and boy was...

My age was irrelevant.

Girl.

Boy.

Did I want more than that?

I didn't. I couldn't. My life was too full to have more.

A week of being a woman.

That was my wish.

That absurd thought made me smile. A wish was defined as a strong desire for something that is not easily attainable, something that cannot or probably will not happen.

Lena Montgomery didn't make wishes. She got shit done.

This felt different.

Maybe for one week...I could be a normal woman, a woman with a wish.

As long as CJ didn't have a dead-fish fetish, it was worth a try.

Why did I agree?

The simple answer was I wanted to. I chose the treadmill beside CJ to give him another chance. I almost slid into *the* Lena mode and made the first move. Why? Because, holy shit, when he turned my way, his handsome face took my breath away. His smile with one dimple. His hair was pulled back as it had been yesterday. I almost blurted out my name, but then he spoke, and I wanted to see where it would go.

As he spoke, I fought images of pulling the hair tie and releasing his dark mane. Thoughts of his unshaved cheeks on my sensitive skin caused my insides to twist. Thank goodness for the sports bra. My nipples would probably have been a dead giveaway.

The loofah sponge caressed my skin, filling the shower stall with the scent of my eucalyptus body-wash. Closing my eyes, I imagined CJ.

How long had it been since I'd been with a man?

It would seem as if I should recall.

I couldn't.

I didn't consider myself loose. I was a modern woman who enjoyed physical pleasure. The giver didn't matter as long as they didn't work for me. Honestly, there were a few friends with benefits in my life. Most likely the last time was with one of them. Our relationships didn't revolve around sex. Sex was a biproduct of the relationship. Men had long had similar relationships, why couldn't a woman?

As I stepped from the shower, I realized what I hadn't been doing. I hadn't been thinking about Architech, Montgomery Holdings, the giver of dead fish, or even my sister. Without more than an invitation to breakfast, CJ had accomplished what I hadn't been able to do in months—refocus my thoughts.

As I readied for breakfast, I made a decision. This week was about resting, relaxing, and taking a break from all the balls I had swirling in the air. Jeremy assured me that Montgomery Holdings would survive without my constant oversight. That said, I knew if I was needed, he wouldn't hesitate to get ahold of me.

The truth was I needed a break—wanted one.

A break from being *the* Lena Montgomery.

CJ said he didn't know who I was.

I didn't know him.

After smashing my lips together to coat them with lip balm, I grinned. Pitching from right to left, I watched as the flowing blue sundress with large blue flowers swung. It was like nothing I'd wear to work. The same could be said for the rhinestone sandals on my feet. I'd bought them on a whim.

The woman in the mirror wasn't the powerhouse in the boardroom. My lips weren't painted red, nor had I spritzed my usual Creed Royal Service perfume. With only mascara, lip balm, and cheeks pink from yesterday's sun, I would spend this week simply being Lena.

Chapter Seven

CJ

After speaking with the concierge, I checked my phone one last time for a message from my brother. Silence. That wasn't how it had been. We used to have two to ten different conversations in the works before I finished my workout.

Before putting my phone away, I sent one text message.

"Mom, still in Cancún. Still safe. Plan to leave the resort by myself to see the city. I'll text later."

A smile curled my lips. If breakfast went well and something worked out with Lena, I wouldn't have to torment my mother for excitement. Before I left the suite, my phone rang. I didn't need to see the name.

"Chandler Johns." My mother's voice was stern.

A full-fledged laugh came out. "Mom, I'm razzing

you. I have no plans, none except I'm headed to breakfast."

"Don't do that to me."

"I just wanted to see if you'd respond."

"Respond," she said, "you're going to give me a heart attack."

"You're fifty-five. I don't see that happening."

"Did I tell you about the story on that news program, you know the one where they recreate crimes?"

I peered down at my watch. I had fifteen minutes to make it to breakfast, and I wanted a table before Lena arrived. "I'm sure you did."

"It was a fancy resort...I don't recall the name..."

I was beginning to regret my poke at my mother bear. "I'm sorry, Mom. I'm really fine, and I'm meeting someone for breakfast. So, give Dad my love, and I'll talk to you later."

"Who are you meeting? Please don't go anywhere with anyone you just met. You never know who they could be. People on vacation aren't always real."

That was my plan—to not be totally real. I doubted that I'd fulfill my earlier fantasies with Lena by starting off breakfast telling her my woes and regrets about becoming filthy rich. "Got it, Mom. Bye."

Quickly, I pushed the red icon before she could respond.

Slipping my phone and wallet into the pocket of my swim trunks, I took one last look in the mirror by the door. The surfing cat tank top should probably go. That said, I didn't pack much for this trip, really anything. Only what I could throw into the carry-on at the last second. The resort had multiple stores.

As I debated my clothing choice, it occurred to me that thinking about my clothes was something I rarely did. That was the beauty of starting your own company, no one to answer to, other than Colton. He didn't give a damn unless we were meeting with investors or interviewing employees. Or making a deal to sell...

Fuck the surfing cat.

My t-shirt from yesterday and the clothes I wore to work out were not fit for company. In other words, they needed laundering. That left one option. On the way to breakfast, I made a quick stop at an open shop and found a greenish-blue tank with the name of the resort on the front. Since it mostly matched my swim trunks, I decided it was a win.

As the girl rang up the purchase, I stripped out of the old tank, pulling it over my head. After ripping the tags off, I slid the new shirt on. When our eyes met, she grinned.

"You must really hate that cat shirt." She lifted her eyebrows. "I think it's unique."

Stuffing the old shirt into the bag the other shirt had come in, I handed it to her. "Is there any way you can keep this? I'm supposed to meet someone for breakfast."

"It's against the rules..." Her smile grew. "But I can hold onto it for a couple of hours. I'm off at noon. Come back before then."

"Thank you."

As I started to walk away, she called out, "I hope you get the job."

My forehead furrowed. "The job?"

"Interview? Right? Otherwise, why change the shirt?"

"I guess I want to impress my breakfast guest. No job..." *I'm independently wealthy.* I didn't say that last part.

"She's a lucky lady."

For the first time, I noticed the girl's name tag. With a wink, I said, "Thank you, Rachel. Let's see if she thinks so. I'll see you before noon."

"If the breakfast doesn't work out..."

Hurrying to the infinity-pool restaurant, I thought

about big-boob lady and now Rachel. I wasn't used to women throwing themselves at me. That wasn't completely true. I'd had my run in high school and college, nothing serious. The last ten years have been more work than play. Now, without work I could play, but I wasn't interested in easy prey.

I preferred a challenge...a lioness.

Let the hunt begin.

My flip-flops flapped against the sidewalks as I made my way through the tropical resort. Whether inside or out, palm trees lined the paths. The restaurant I was looking forward to had a view of the Caribbean Sea beyond the pool. Later the restaurant would close, and the pool would open to guests.

A hostess led me to a table for two at the side of the pool. The morning sunlight filtered through the overhead veranda covered in vines with large purple and pink flowers. Large bamboo fans swirled, creating a breeze in the steamy air.

"Coffee?" a man in a shirt with the resort logo asked moments after I sat.

"Yes."

He turned over my cup. "Are you dining alone?"

"I hope not," I confessed.

Instantly, his smile softened, and his eyes took on a new life. "First date. You met here."

"Is it that obvious?"

He looked at my shirt and back to me. "Last minute, you got rid of whatever you were wearing, stopped in a shop, and bought something that matches."

I took a deep breath. "Basically. So since you seem to be an expert, how do these dates, if that's even what it is, work out?"

He shrugged. "If this mystery woman…or is it a man?"

"Woman."

"If she shows, I'll give you a forty percent chance of hooking up."

"I'm not…" My thoughts went to my fantasies. "That's not the only reason I want her to show."

"Who to show?"

The waiter and I both turned as Lena appeared, a breath of fresh air. With the exception of this morning in the gym, this was the first time I saw her face without the large sunglasses and hat. And I was a bit preoccupied with her presence on the treadmill to appreciate her exquisite beauty.

With very little makeup, Lena was stunning.

Her deep red hair was no longer in ringlets, but curled near her chin, and the sundress she wore hid the curves I'd seen at the pool. Yet the spaghetti straps revealed her slender shoulders and collarbone, the way the V formed at the base of her neck. Large blue earrings dangled near her shoulders and reflected the sun.

Quickly, I stood and motioned toward the other chair.

The waiter stepped in and pulled the chair back.

Hanging a large bag from the chair, Lena sat, turning her mesmerizing, soft brown gaze on me.

I answered her question. "You, if you showed, and you did."

"I believe I was invited."

"You were," I said, taking my seat.

The waiter spoke to Lena. "May I get you a coffee?"

"I was promised coffee and mimosas."

Flipping over her cup, he turned to me and winked. "Mimosas for two?"

"Yes."

"Here are the menus." He lowered two cardboard rectangles that I hadn't noticed before. "I'll be back with the coffee and mimosas." Before he walked away, he whispered, "Eighty."

Eighty percent chance.

I grinned.

"Eighty?" Lena inquired after he was gone.

"The high today...yes, it's supposed to be eighty."

"Really? I'd guess higher."

A grin took over my face. "I can only hope."

She took a deep breath and looked around. "It seems we have one of the best tables."

I wanted to blurt out a thousand questions and an hour-long dissertation on myself, and yet words were escaping me. The silence settled, easing the unfamiliarity as I confessed my thoughts. "I meant what I said in the gym."

Lena brought the glass of iced water to her lips. "Are you reminding me that you're a predator, CJ?"

I liked the sound of my name on her lips. "If I'm any good at reading people, we have a ways to go to determine who rules in that category."

"I'm a woman. Wouldn't you assume it's you?"

"Call me intrigued, Lena. My vision is better than twenty-twenty. I'm well aware that you're a woman. I also don't believe in assuming."

She grinned and after taking a drink, set the water glass back on the table. "Tell me what you meant in the gym."

"You are the woman I saw yesterday at the pool bar, the woman I couldn't stop thinking about."

Chapter Eight

Lena

"I remember," I said as my cheeks warmed. "I thought you might come over to my lounge chair yesterday."

"I wanted to." CJ shook his head. "Without going into detail, I'm here, in Cancún, because I wanted to get away. Yesterday when I arrived, I realized that I was wrong. I'm ashamed to admit I spent a great deal of yesterday wallowing. You were the highlight of yesterday, Lena. Thinking about you reminded me that life can go on. I can go on."

"Don't tell me this was supposed to be your honeymoon or something. No woman would leave you at the altar."

CJ scoffed. "Since I've never been to the altar, the

jury is out on that one. No, my wallowing was my own doing and had nothing to do with a woman."

Our waiter arrived with two mimosas and a pot of coffee. Setting the champagne glasses before us, he proceeded to fill our coffee cups. "Have you decided what you'd like to order."

I looked around for a buffet but didn't see one.

"May we have some more time?" I asked.

"You're in paradise. Take as long as you'd like."

Nodding, I reached for the slender glass.

CJ lifted his and extended it toward me. "To you, Lena, and to focusing on the present."

"And to you too." Our glasses clinked before we both took a sip.

The champagne bubbles tickled my throat.

I tilted my head to the side. "Does that toast mean you don't want to talk about what brought you here, what you were wallowing in?"

"It does." His turquoise stare was on me. "It means the gods have shown me a beautiful woman, and I can't turn down a gift from the gods. Real life won't go away if I take a break."

The gods.

"I've been called many things," I said with a grin. "A gift from the gods is a new one."

When CJ didn't respond, I thought about the rest of his sentence.

A break.

"Is that what you want, a break?" I asked.

"What do you want, Lena?"

Sitting back, I inhaled and pulled my gaze away from CJ's and out to the crystal blue waters beyond the pool. Returning my eyes to his, I answered, "I don't know. As you said, real life isn't going anywhere. I'm not accustomed to this..."

"The resort is amazing," he said, "and pricey."

"Yes, that's not really what I meant. I'm not accustomed to relaxing. If I must confess, I'm a workaholic. After intervention from those close to me, I was convinced, or coerced, into booking a real vacation, a holiday away from..." I wasn't ready to share the list.

"Real life," CJ said, finishing my thought.

"In a nutshell."

The menu caught my attention. Lifting it, I read the options. "Have you decided what you're going to order?"

"It depends."

"On?"

"Are you the carnivore you claimed to be?"

My grin grew. "My meal choice won't give that away."

"So, you won't be having sausage with a side of bacon?"

I shook my head. "Not because that doesn't sound...well, it sounds a little too much, but no, because a friend of mine convinced me to bring a two-piece bathing suit, and I want it to fit when I go back to my suite."

"Please thank your friend for me." Heat simmered in his gaze. "I memorized that swimsuit."

Before I could respond, the waiter came for our orders and to refill our coffee. If we could determine prey from predator by our breakfast order, CJ would win. My yogurt and fruit with granola lacked the protein in his omelet with a side of bacon.

The style of shirt he was wearing revealed his shoulders and muscular arms. I doubted that he worried about caloric intake, especially not the way he was running on the treadmill. A giggle escaped my lips.

"What's funny?"

"Your shirt. I just realized it has the name of the resort."

He leaned back and looked down at the shirt, the same color as his eyes. When he looked up, his dimple was on full display. "I didn't put a lot of thought into packing."

"If you bought that for me, for this breakfast, don't. I don't care about your clothes."

His eyes opened wide as I realized what I'd said. "I mean, I want you to wear clothes..."

As the awkwardness of this conversation continued, so did the deep chuckle of CJ's laugh.

When my cheeks were sufficiently warmed, CJ leaned forward, his broad shoulders over the table and his volume low. "I've been imagining you without them."

I wanted to say that I'd been doing the same. Instead, I narrowed my gaze. "What did you think?"

He moved his eyebrows. "About you naked? I approved."

"I'm a firm believer in equality. If I'm without clothes..."

"I'm game." He began to stand, offering me his hand. "Shall we?"

Leaning back, I shook my head with a smile. "You, sir, offered me breakfast."

He retook his seat. "If I recall it was coffee and mimosas." He waved his hand over the table. "Mission accomplished."

"Remember what I said about being prey?"

"There's nothing about you that suggests you're prey, Lena. On the contrary, you are an enigma."

"Is that so?" I asked.

My skin warmed with the heat of his stare as if he were studying me. "You are the lioness, sleek, stunningly beautiful, and majestic. You exude confidence. I imagine whatever you do, you do well. And yet you blush when I compliment you. As if there are two amazing women in one. I want to know more about each one."

"You determined all of that from the gym and these few minutes?"

"Would you think I'm a stalker if I told you I watched you yesterday, wondering if you'd come back to the bar."

My spine straightened at his choice of words. "You watched me?"

The waiter arrived with our food. Once he was gone, CJ lifted his fork. "Saved by the waiter."

"One of us was." I lowered my spoon into the soft, creamy yogurt. When I looked up, his gaze was on me. "I'm not about taking things slow," I confessed.

His dimple reappeared. "Take charge."

I shrugged. "This is one week. I'd like to see where it leads."

"And I'd like to see you..." His words trailed away as his dimple grew deeper.

I had a million questions.

What does he do?

Why does he need a break?

Why did he say at the gym that he regretted being the predator?

And yet I asked none of them. Because my questions would lead to questions from him, questions I didn't want to answer, subjects I didn't want to cloud my thoughts. Instead, I chose to live in the present. With the gentle breeze from the fans above and the din of the ocean beyond the pool, I would soak up the here and now.

"I wanted to go to your chair yesterday," he said, breaking the silence. "I just had to get out of my own head."

"Are you out?"

CJ nodded.

"Then maybe you'd like to join me today?"

"I reserved a cabana on the beach."

My eyes widened. "Confident?"

"Hopeful."

"And if I hadn't shown for breakfast?"

"I'd have a cabana all to myself, which doesn't sound as fun as sharing it with you."

"I want to share it with you." I lowered my spoon. "I want a break too." Pausing, I gave my next sentence some thought. "Please don't take this wrong."

He leaned back as his hands dropped to his sides. "That is never a good start to a conversation."

"It's not the start. It's the middle."

"Go on."

Inhaling, I met his gaze. "I'm not married or anything like that."

CJ's eyes widened. "Good to know. I'm not either."

"I figured. No ring."

"You either."

"I'm only looking for a break from reality. Real life needs me to return."

"One week."

I nodded and lifted my champagne glass. "To us. To a week to remember, one that hopefully makes us each smile once we return to real life."

With a sexy grin, CJ lifted his glass. "A week with you will be impossible to forget."

Chapter Nine

Lena

There was an indescribable elation the moment when all the pieces of a business deal came together. It was the moment when the late nights, hours of research, and lack of sleep all culminated into the perfect storm—the lucrative payoff. Whether it was the gotcha moment when securing an acquisition or the satisfaction with turning a company that was in the red to the black, that was the feeling I lived for.

I sought out opportunities.

I'd learned early in my quest of attainment that life didn't present breaks on a silver platter. It was the digging, the pursuit, and the willingness to learn that separated the winners from the losers. I had an affinity for start-ups. That road map had paid handsomely in the past.

However, staring across the table as our champagne glasses clinked, I had a different sensation, something I'd not allowed myself to entertain.

New.

Engaging.

Endearing.

Giving myself a week's hiatus, I could possibly grow to adore this unusual and different feeling.

It was the way CJ looked at me.

Much like the feeling of the great deal, as I sipped my mimosa, something tingled through me. Electricity bringing life back to a basic part of me I had kept dormant for most of my adulthood. I wouldn't lie to myself and make this any bigger than it was.

I barely knew the man with his gaze upon me.

We weren't in love or even in like.

This was lust with a side of curiosity.

If I ever learned his secrets or he mine, we both may run in different directions.

This was attraction.

The kind of lure that pulled me toward him, wanting his companionship. Not for a big deal. Not for forever. It was as if there was a magnetic pull, one that I felt the first time we spoke at the bar. With each moment in his presence, the allure grew stronger, as if there was more—a silver lining—so to speak.

"Where are you from?" CJ asked as we resumed eating.

"All over."

"Oh, come on. There is somewhere you call home."

A blueberry covered in yogurt sat on my spoon. "Currently, Missoula, Montana."

"I've heard that's the new Silicon Valley."

"Not quite, but it's beautiful with a side of tech." I grinned. "What about you?"

He shrugged his broad shoulders. "Originally from Ohio. Nothing wrong with it, but I wanted out."

"So where is out?"

"Lately, it's been in Austin." His expression dimmed. "I guess I'm not sure anymore." He winked. "I could check out Missoula."

"Is this part of why you were in your head?"

Lifting his napkin, CJ wiped his lips and sat back. "It is and since I made my way out, I'd like to stay here in your company."

"So, rule number one," I said, "no discussing real life."

CJ's smile was back. "You're a rule follower."

"I never said that."

"Then why make rules?"

I tweaked an eyebrow. "For you to follow."

"I see," he said with a laugh. "You're the rule maker."

Finishing off my mimosa, I gave his comment some thought. I did make rules. I set boundaries, I planned to the nth, I also broke rules. I'd done worse than break rules, and in hindsight, I felt no regret for the lengths I'd traveled. Along the way I'd made mistakes, serious life-altering mistakes. With each mistake, I learned. I dusted myself off. I moved forward. In the grand scheme of life, I'd come out ahead.

"Yes," I finally answered. "I'm better at making rules than following them."

"Now you're talking. A rule breaker."

"You?"

CJ looked at our empty dishes and glasses seconds before the waiter appeared.

"May I get you both another mimosa?" he asked.

"How about a walk on the beach?" CJ asked.

Nodding, I smiled at the waiter. "Thank you. We can put this on my room."

"All-inclusive," CJ said. "Any additional charges will go on my suite."

A few minutes later the waiter was back and handed the small black folder to CJ.

"Wait," I said. "You don't need to pay for—"

CJ waved as he signed his name and suite number.

Once the waiter was gone, I pressed my lips together and narrowed my gaze.

When CJ noticed, he began to laugh. Standing, he offered me his hand. "Come on, Lena. You are obviously capable. For this week, could you allow me to pamper you?"

"Pamper?"

"One week, remember. Then it's back to real life. Tell me, who pampers you in real life?"

I laid my hand in his. As his long fingers encased my hand, a tingling sensation radiated from my palm in his grasp throughout my body. Looking up to his handsome face, I stood, feeling the warmth of his touch and the nearness of his body. For longer than either of us intended, we stood in the middle of the outdoor restaurant, near the infinity pool, and stared. His eyes with the colors of the ocean swirled with emotions. As the silence prevailed and the world beyond our two-person bubble faded, we reached out to one another in ways words were insufficient to express.

For one week I wanted to learn more about this man—the one who made me forget my long list of concerns and the one who had awakened a primal part of me. That feminine part of me hoped CJ wanted the same thing.

Moistening my lips, I tried to recall what he'd said.

"Pampering," CJ prompted.

"I'd say any pampering is by my own hand."

His smile quirked and his dimple came into view. "Not this week. This week all the pampering will come from me." He leaned closer to my ear and whispered, "Pleasure too."

As he spoke, his warm breath tickled my skin.

"Only if it's a two-way street."

Before we could make our way to the beach, I saw Adam leaning against one of the tiki-style bars, his eyes on us.

"Just a minute," I said as I stepped into a shaded area and removed my phone from the large purse. In no time at all, I sent a text to Adam and Kelsey.

"No dead fish. Give us space."

I knew better than to ask them for privacy. Involving themselves in my private life was what the members of my security did, what I paid them to do. Space seemed to be a happy medium.

Tossing my phone back into my purse, I grinned and reached for CJ's arm. "To the beach."

As we stepped onto the soft white sand, I removed my sandals, adding them to my bag. CJ took off his leather flip-flops and held them in one hand while he captured my hand with his other. My feet sank into the warm sand as we passed the cabanas and headed toward the shore.

"I forget there are so many shades of blue," I said as the breeze blew my hair around my face and my sundress fluttered in the wind.

"This is my first time here."

Like it was meant to be.

"It's one of my favorite seas," I said. "The Mediterranean is stunning too, especially in Greece."

CJ's steps came to a stop, and he looked down at me. With both of us having bare feet, CJ was easily seven or eight inches taller. "You must travel a lot."

"Not usually for pleasure. Work."

"I'm glad you got your boss to give you a free week."

My boss.

When I looked up, I nodded. "It was a hard sell, but she went for it." We began walking again until our feet were washed in waves of warm, salty water. "Was it difficult for you to get time away?" I asked.

"Nah, I'm kind of between gigs."

For the next few minutes, we walked the shoreline. I wasn't certain of how far we'd gone or where we were until we came to a sign indicating the property line for the resort. The beach beyond this point was barren, seaweed near the water. What was manicured farther from the shore was now filled with sea grapes and tall grasses. Even though CJ kept walking, I stopped.

"You don't want to keep walking?" he asked.

Shaking my head, I tried to shrug off the sudden sense of dread. Turning around, I looked back for Adam and Kelsey. If they were watching, they were giving me the space I'd demanded. Despite my spike in pulse, I tried to make my voice light. "Let's head back."

"It's not as if there's an invisible fence. We can walk beyond this point." CJ demonstrated by walking forward a few feet and back. As he did, the breeze picked up, the sea grapes rustled, and grasses swayed.

"The resort is secure," I reasoned.

"Lena, are you okay?" He again took my hand. "I was just joking about the fence. If you want to go back, we can go back."

Though CJ was talking, my focus stayed on the sea grapes, wondering if I'd seen someone hiding behind the foliage.

"Lena?"

"What?" I turned to CJ.

At the same time, a young couple came running out of the hedges.

"Oh," I yelped.

My entire body stiffened as my skin chilled. It didn't matter that the sun was beating down or that the young couple was giggling, the strings of the girl's bikini flying in her wake. Even as I watched the woman peering over her shoulder, egging the man on toward the water, the breakfast I'd eaten churned in my stomach.

"You're white as a sheet," CJ said.

My gaze went down to where our hands were connected and back to him. "Let's go back to the resort. You rented a cabana. We shouldn't waste it."

When we turned, in the distance, I saw a couple walking our direction. With the glare of the sun, it was difficult to make out the details. Yet I knew. Breathing a sigh of relief, I knew it was Adam and Kelsey.

It wasn't until we grew closer to the couple that my bodyguards turned and walked ahead of us.

As much as I hated being smothered, I had to admit, I was happy they were near.

Our walk back was filled with small talk about beaches and weather. While this was CJ's first trip to Cancún, he had done some traveling, mostly around the US. He compared the white sand to that of western Florida, telling me that his grandparents have a place down there, and when he was younger, his spring breaks were spent visiting.

I acknowledged his story and encouraged him to keep talking, but my mind was on the rustling sea grapes, the sudden paralyzing fear that we'd been followed. Every few minutes, I would peer over at the man still holding my hand.

Had he taken me that way on purpose?

Could he be working with my fish stalker?

No.

It was my imagination.

The real reason for this getaway.

The reason I'd left Missoula in a rush.

The attempt on my life.

"I can walk you to your room and you can change, and we'll come back to the cabana."

His words barely registered as I looked up at the large resort. Seeing it from afar made me realize how large it was, how my stalker could so easily be there. It hadn't seemed that large while I was inside or on the pool deck. But out here...

Chapter Ten

CJ

There was something melancholy in Lena's expression that emanated a wave of sadness. Even with her eyes hidden behind large sunglasses, I felt a chill as if she'd left me, going someplace she didn't want to be. Reaching for her chin, I turned her gaze to mine. "What thoughts are going through your beautiful mind?"

As she inhaled, her neck and shoulders straightened. "CJ, this isn't a good time for me."

"With me? Walking on the beach or is it bigger than that?"

"Bigger. Much bigger."

Still holding her face, I leaned closer until my lips met hers. Soft and firm, she didn't back away or hesitate to return my kiss. When it ended, I grinned and placed another kiss on her forehead. The return of her smile was radiant.

"One week," I said. "Let the bigger go for one week. I won't pry. I just want to do what I can to see you smile."

She nodded. "Remember what you said you were doing yesterday?"

"Wallowing?"

"In your own head. I was just there."

"I missed you while you were gone."

Her cheeks rose and her head tilted. "You're not real."

Taking her hand, I placed her palm on my chest. "I'm real, Lena. Flesh and blood, beating heart."

"Physically you're real. I've known a lot of men. You're too good to be true."

I shrugged. "I've been rather preoccupied for" —I wanted to say forever— "many years. I don't have a vast history of relationships. I don't know what's real and what's not real. I know you have a gorgeous smile that I'd like to see more often. I enjoy hearing your voice and your laugh. I fucking want more of your lips and whatever else I can get."

Pink filled her cheeks.

"And it's my goal to make you blush."

"I don't blush."

"You do. You are."

Lena's hands went to her cheeks as she nodded. "Okay. One week. I'll try to stay out of my own head, and you do the same."

Taking her hand, I shook it. "Deal."

"Which cabana did you rent?"

"They said it would have a sign."

Together we walked around the large cabanas until we found the one with the sign that read *CJ*. On the ground level was a soft mattress surrounded by straw mats and flowing curtains. Up a small ladder was a sundeck with two chairs. To the side was a cooler. I'd had it filled with water bottles. "We will also have an attendant and can order whatever we'd like." I looked toward the resort. "And the pool bars are up there, if we want anything else." I bowed at the waist. "I'm here for your pampering."

Lena's smile shone as she walked around the circumference of the cabana and ran her fingers over the curtains. Her blue sundress hung to her calves, and her bare feet left her footprints in the sand. Her finger- and toenails matched, colored in pale blue. I was drawn to her dichotomy. Physically, she was petite, lean with curves in all the right places—almost fragile. For a moment when she was in her head, I sensed vulnerability. And yet yesterday and today at breakfast, she seemed the exact opposite.

The lioness was returning.

Her grin grew. "This is much more secluded than the pool."

"That was my plan."

She let out a breath. "I'll go change and meet you back here."

"I can walk with you."

"Then you'd know my suite number."

"That was also my plan."

"How about we take your plan one step at a time?"

"You drive a hard bargain."

She grinned. "It's kind of what I do."

"I'll let you go," I said, "under one condition."

Her eyebrows rose above her sunglasses. "You'll *let* me?"

I tilted my head to the side and flashed my best smile. Yes, the lioness was back, and I was quickly becoming addicted to her spirit. "Yes."

She pursed her lips as her fists came to her sides. "What is your condition?"

"That you let me kiss you again."

After a moment of deliberate calculation, she nodded. "I can live with that."

I took a step closer. "A real kiss."

"Was the last one not real?" Lifting her chin, she stood her ground as I snaked my arms around her waist.

"You're something else, Lena."

Her hands came to my shoulders. "I'm not the prey." She pushed up on her tiptoes as her lips met mine.

The sounds of the surf and din of other beachgoers disappeared as we both took and gave in equal proportions. My face tilted to deepen the kiss as her soft body molded against my hard one. My tongue sought entrance first, quickly followed by hers. Twirling around and around, soft mews filled my ears.

Lena's hands moved higher to my hair.

When our kiss ended, she stared up at me. "That was a real kiss."

"Then I guess that was my one condition."

She opened her hand and showed me the hair tie she'd tugged from my hair. "This is yours." As I reached for it, she closed her fingers. "I've wanted to do that since I saw you at the bar."

Running my fingers through my now-free-flowing hair, I smirked. "Are you going to give it back?"

"Nope." She took a step back. "Not until I return and find you here. It's my insurance policy to be sure you don't stand me up."

Stand her up.

The thought never entered my mind.

"I can't imagine you ever being stood up."

"Or you," she said, peering over her slender shoulder.

I stood watching as she walked toward the resort. The slight sway of her round ass and the way she carried herself told me that her confidence was back. What I didn't know was why it had waned. It had seemed as if she were genuinely upset that we'd reached the property line of the resort.

Recalling my mother's fears, I considered that perhaps Lena had similar concerns, having heard stories of terror and doom. If that were the case, I'd spend this week ensuring that she was safe, that the lioness was in all her glory.

As I was about to get a bottle of water, I looked up, seeing a man approach Lena near the pool.

My shoulders straightened and my heart beat faster. Without thinking, I took off toward the pool. In the seconds it took for me to get there, they were both gone. I stood on the concrete with my hair dangling near my jaw, looking in all directions. The resort had multiple buildings, pools, and shops. I had no idea which building held her suite.

Shit.

Why didn't we exchange numbers?

"Señor, may I help you?"

The waiter was one I'd seen yesterday.

"There was just a woman here. She was in a blue dress. Auburn hair. Big sunglasses. She was carrying a white bag."

The waiter nodded. "Sí, I saw her. I believe she left with her husband."

Her husband?

"No, she isn't married." At least that's what she'd said.

"I'm sorry. I don't know for sure. She greeted him by name. Adam. Yes, that was his name."

Who the fuck is Adam?

"Okay," I mumbled. "Thanks."

"Sí, may I get you anything?"

Well, fuck. Maybe I was the one about to be stood up. I turned toward the beach and pointed to the cabana I'd rented for the day. "I'm in cabana six. Could someone bring out a bottle of champagne on ice. Two glasses."

"Sí. Two?"

"Yes."

As I turned back toward the beach, I decided I would either learn about Adam and who he is to Lena, or if she didn't come back, I'd drink the champagne double fisted. The warm breeze from the sea blew my hair back as I lifted my chin.

Reaching for my hair tie, I realized it wasn't on my wrist. No, Lena took it.

She'd be back.

Back out at the cabana, I pulled my new shirt over my head and tossed it onto the mattress.

Do I have time to go get the shirt I left at the store?

If I hurried.

Chapter Eleven

Lena

As we made our way to my suite, I told Adam about the couple in the sea grapes. I wasn't sure why I told him. The time was past. The couple was benign, but the truth was the situation frightened me. The fact it affected me the way it did made me mad.

"We need to learn who's responsible for the poison and the fish," I said after he made sure the suite was clear.

"They're working on it back in Montana. That's why you're here."

Inhaling, I closed my eyes. Exhaling, I said, "Come in while I change."

Adam stepped inside the suite, securing the door

behind him. "Ma'am, there are only a few people who know your location. The airplane rental was done under a rarely used shell company. Other than Mr. Wilde, your assistant Gigi, and Montgomery security, no one knows."

"I hate this," I confessed. Letting my hands drop to my sides, I spun around the living room area of the suite. Beyond the French doors was a balcony with a private pool and the Caribbean Ocean sparkling to the horizon. "I'm not prey."

"Ma'am?"

"I'm not prey. That's not who I am."

Adam nodded in agreement.

"Whoever this is," I confessed, "they're getting to me. They're in my head, and it makes me question what I shouldn't question."

"Like what?"

"Like could CJ have purposely taken me down the beach to the property line." I shook my head and tossed my large bag onto the sofa. "I don't want to think that way about him." I shrugged. "I like him."

Adam's eyes opened wide as his eyebrow rose.

"I know," I replied. "I just met him. I want to trust him, only for this week. But what about the opposite? What if him being with me even for a week puts him in danger?"

"Kelsey said you don't want us to do a background check."

"I didn't." I shook my head. "No, I still don't want to know more about him than what I learn from him. It's the fish stalker. It's that he went further than stalking when he sent the poisoned candy."

"He?"

"I'm assuming it's a man. You know I think it could be Logan Butler."

Adam shook his head. "We haven't ruled him out. There's no doubt he knows it was you who stepped in with the SPAC and the grand jury indictment with his brother's investments. However, we have no proof of him being in Missoula. Our people say he's in Chicago."

"What about Phillip?" Phillip was my brother-in-law, my sister's husband. "I know he's in prison. Could he have a connection?"

"We've spoken with the warden. It's unlikely."

I sat on the arm of the sofa. "I should be thinking about the sexy man waiting for me at the beach, and instead, I'm racking my brain about who would hate me enough to do this." My gaze met Adam's. "It's personal. Violating my home and attempting my demise."

Leaning against the wall, Adam crossed his ankles

and sighed. "I'd like to do a background check on CJ. If it comes back clear, I won't say a word. You'll know he's safe or seems safe. If I find any red flags, I'll tell you."

Nodding, I looked down at my lap and back up, my focus on the man I trusted with my safety. "I don't want to know any information other than" —I inhaled — "if there's any reason to think CJ could be connected to my stalker."

"For the record, men are usually more direct with their threats. Women are more likely to use poison."

Over twenty years ago, Logan had been more direct.

My sister poisoned some people. She'd also used a weapon.

In other words, patterns were present to be broken.

I asked, "Are you saying that you think the stalker is a woman?"

"Ms. Montgomery, we don't know. Whoever this is, he or she is very careful. The note that came with the candy was handwritten. The writing is being analyzed. The postmark was Missoula."

My stomach twisted.

This person was in the same city as me or as where I lived.

"Won't they see that I'm not in town, not going to the office?"

"Yes," Adam answered. "You aren't there. No one can track you here."

Standing, I brushed the front of my sundress. "I'm going to change into my bathing suit and cover-up. Were you able to secure a cabana near cabana number six?"

"Kelsey is already there. We're in fourteen. It's about twenty yards away. We can see the back of number six. We'll be watching everyone who gets close."

I let out a long sigh. "Thank you. Thank you for caring—for doing your job."

"We care." His lips curled into a smile. "Relax. If I learn anything alarming, we'll interrupt."

Less than ten minutes later, I was wearing a bathing suit and beach cover. Adam and I were headed back to the cabana.

"We can part ways at the pool," he suggested.

"I have my phone."

"And your watch," he said with a grin. "All you know is C.J.?"

"Yes, as far as a name. It's all that was written on the sign reserving the cabana. I also know that he's originally from Ohio. Currently lives in Austin."

"Do you know his profession?"

"No, but he doesn't know mine either. He said he

was between gigs." I furrowed my brow. "Hell, maybe he's in entertainment." I thought about that. "Oh, the last thing I need is to be involved with some famous band member that will get my picture on social media. If that's it, tell me."

"Yes, ma'am."

As I walked across the warm sand toward the cabana, I knew talking to Adam helped clear my mind. I was being watched, protected. I didn't want to be told about CJ, but it would ease my anxiousness to learn he wasn't a threat.

That didn't mean I wasn't a threat to him.

Stepping around the flowing curtains, my smile returned. The turquoise of the ocean paled in comparison to the gaze now scanning me, from my wide-brimmed hat to my toes. I knew CJ worked out, or at least ran, but seeing him in only his swim trunks was a beautiful sight. With his hair untethered, it curled near his chiseled jawline. His shoulders were broad and muscles defined, including the six- or eight-pack of abs. The muscles didn't stop there, visible in his long legs.

"You came back."

Hearing his deep voice brought back memories of our kiss.

Removing the hair tie from my wrist, I extended it

toward the sexy, shirtless man on the mattress. "I believe this is yours."

CJ patted the mattress beside him. "And this spot is yours."

Next to the mattress within the cabana was an ice bucket on a stand and a small table with two champagne flutes.

"I don't remember seeing that earlier."

"Because it wasn't here. I figured we'd share, or if you stood me up, I would go back to plan A."

"Plan A?"

"Wallowing."

I scoffed. "Plan B?"

"A week with no bigger worries."

"I like that." Feeling the need to explain my extended absence, I added, "I had to discuss something with someone. I didn't mean to make you think I wouldn't return."

"I was hopeful." He lifted the hair tie. "Your insurance policy and all."

Laying my beach bag on the straw mat, I knelt on the side of the mattress and peered out toward the ocean. "This is nice."

"And private."

My gaze met CJ's as I unbuttoned the front of my beach cover-up. One by one. His breathing deepened as his eyes stayed glued to the progressive opening. Soon I was standing in only my bikini.

"You are so beautiful."

"Back atcha."

CJ sat taller. "No, Lena. You're stunning."

"I'm glad you think so."

He lifted his chin. "Come here." It wasn't a request, and yet I didn't mind.

As soon as I lay back against the inclined mattress, CJ leaned closer and removed my sunglasses. Cupping my cheek with his large palm, he didn't hesitate to bring his lips to mine. My core twisted with need at his ability to kiss.

Kissing was an underrated skill, and if I were to give CJ's ability a grade, it would be A+. His lips and tongue fit perfectly with mine. His warmth raising the temperature within me from simmering to boiling, in seconds I was lost as he unapologetically took what I was willing to give.

My palms teased over his arms and shoulders, feeling the definition I'd ogled moments earlier. As his wide chest pressed against my breasts, my hunger for him grew, causing my nipples to bead.

Without forethought, my fingers weaved through his dark mane.

The heat in his touch was everywhere, running his

hands over my arms and shoulders and finally down my side, caressing my breast and moving down to my thigh. We struggled for air as we devoured one another, both starving for more of what was right here. I tipped my head up as his lips moved lower.

Nips and kisses peppered my skin. Down my neck, over my collarbone, between my breasts.

Chapter Twelve

CJ

Lena tasted like sunshine on a cloudy day. That one ray that reached through the clouds as a reminder that the storm would pass. With all her talk of being the aggressor, she was sensual and so fucking responsive.

My questions about Adam disappeared the moment Lena came around the side of the cabana. I'd never claimed to have the ability to read people, but that beautiful smile didn't belong to a woman actively cheating on her husband—a husband who was here at this resort.

As she unbuttoned her cover-up, I was mesmerized, wanting her to continue disrobing. Alas, she stopped at the cover-up, her bathing suit still in place.

Now, as I lowered myself, kissing and nipping her

flawless skin, I teased the edge of her bathing suit top. Pushing the material away, I took her nipple between my lips, swirling the hardened bead with my tongue.

Her fingers in my hair held me in place as I released her other breast. Moans and sounds came from her lips as her body fidgeted below mine with need.

It was as if we were alone on a desert island, not in a cabana at a large resort.

Lifting my head, I met her light-chocolate gaze. "Tell me to stop. I won't want to, but I will."

Her pink lips curled upward. "If I wanted you to stop, you'd know." Palming my cheeks, she reached for my chin and tugged me toward her. When our noses were close, she asked, "Do you think they know what people do in these secluded cabanas?"

Lowering my timbre, I asked, "What do you want to do in this secluded cabana?"

"Exactly what we're doing."

"It's a start, but I want more."

Lena nodded. "I do too."

I ran my thumb over her lips, pinkened from our kissing.

Laying the mattress back, I resumed my exploration, meticulously lavishing each and every inch of exposed flesh with my attention. Goose bumps came to life, and Lena's back arched as I nipped and sucked her hard nipples.

My dick hardened as I trailed my lips down her stomach.

With her legs parted, I kissed the insides of her thighs.

Her arousal was sweet, dampening the material covering her core.

For the first time in recent history, my thoughts were consumed with something other than Architech. As Lena writhed beneath my adoration, I wanted nothing more than to please her. Brushing my nose against the crotch of her swimsuit, I inhaled.

Peering upward, I saw her stare on mine. "I want to taste you."

Her tits moved up and down as her breathing deepened. Nodding, she replied, "I want that too." Her focus changed from me to the ocean and back to me. "We aren't alone. Public indecency isn't on my bucket list."

She was right.

Tilting my head, I smiled. "Private indecency has moved up my list."

Lena grinned. "I don't want us to end up in a video on some social-media platform."

Pulling myself over her, I lowered my lips, giving

each of her round tits a last kiss before tucking them back into their assigned cups. When I looked up, I saw her pout.

"When I take you," I said, my tenor deep and my cadence steady, "I want you to have the privacy and freedom to scream my name." I grinned. "And I want the freedom to see all of you without either of us wondering if anyone else can see."

"*When* you take me?"

Moving back to where her lips were close enough to kiss, I nodded. "Yes, when."

As I crawled up the mattress beside her, the tenting of my swim trunks was on full display.

Lena's cheeks took on a rosy hue as she spoke. "I want the privacy to help you with your current situation."

The mental image of Lena on her knees had me on the verge of coming.

Her hand lowered to the front of my suit, pressing and running her palm over my erection. Despite my already-hardened state, under her touch, my dick went from wood to steel, and my balls tightened. My arousal was due to more than her touch, but also the way her chocolate stare stayed fixed on me. This woman was every bit the lioness I presumed. Yes, she'd accept pleasure—on her terms. Giving pleasure would be on her terms as well.

Taking her hand away, I brought it to my lips and kissed her palm. "Fuck, Lena. This cabana was a bad idea."

After a chaste kiss and readjusting her lounge, she sat back and sighed. "It's not a bad idea." Her smile was stunning. "However, it isn't completely achieving our goal."

"What was our goal again?"

Her gaze sparkled with the reflection of the sun beyond our curtains. "Big issues. I'm most definitely thinking about what appears to be a particularly large issue at the moment."

"Come with me to my suite. If you don't want me to know your suite number, I want you to know mine."

She turned her attention back to the ocean. "I'm not saying no. I'm just not saying yes, not yet."

I turned to the ice bucket covered in condensation. "Then let's have a toast to not yet."

Standing, I pulled the bottle from the ice and began the task of removing the wire cage to free the cork.

"I know we said no discussing real life," she said, "but I've been thinking about something you said about being between gigs."

Turning toward the ocean, I twisted the cork until it popped with a bang and champagne bubbled from the spout.

"That was loud," she said with a giggle as a man and a woman hurried around the cabana, their eyes fixed on me.

"Champagne," Lena explained.

The man's stance relaxed as the woman apologized for the interruption.

"We're fine," I offered, setting the bottle back in the ice and looking closer at the man. "Adam?"

"Sir?"

"This is Adam, right?" I asked Lena.

She sat up. "How would you know his name?"

"Are you two" —I looked from Lena to Adam— "married?"

"No."

There was a silent stare-off that I wasn't a part of. Nevertheless, my questions continued. "But you know one another?"

Shaking her head, Lena reached for her beach cover and stood, slipping her feet into her sandals. "Thank you for a nice morning, CJ. Perhaps plan A is the way to go."

"What the fuck is happening?"

The brunette woman again apologized for interrupting, but my attention was on Lena. As she picked up her white bag and hat and began walking toward the open curtains, I stepped in front of her, my chest blocking her way. "Tell me what just happened, how we went from one hundred to zero in a matter of seconds."

Before my words were out, Adam's hand was on my shoulder.

I spun toward him, breaking his grip. "Excuse me." We met eye to eye. I didn't intend to fight this man, but I would. He looked fit, but I was too, and I had youth on my side.

"Adam, it's all right." Lena took a deep breath. "This is Adam Dillon and Kelsey Nicholson." She turned to Adam and Kelsey. "This is CJ."

Adam and Kelsey nodded.

"What is this?" I asked. "Some swinging thing?"

Lena shook her head with a laugh. "No. This is my life, CJ. Adam and Kelsey work for me. They're my security detail."

Wait. What?

"You have a security detail? Are you famous or something?"

"More like something."

"You're saying that when you left the pool with

him" —I tilted my head toward Adam— "it was because he's your bodyguard?"

"You were out here. How did you know I left the pool with Adam?"

"I followed you. I wanted to be sure you were all right. You seemed to be freaked out during our walk and after." The pieces were clicking into place. "You were freaked out." My eyes narrowed. "You were afraid. That's why you have them."

Lena lowered the bag to the mattress and turned toward her bodyguards. "I'm not ready to leave. Please go."

"Go?" I asked. "Aren't they supposed to be sure you're safe?"

"Am I not safe with you?"

"No, you are." I ran my hand through my hair. "Are you royalty?"

"Please," she said to them as they both walked away. When her eyes came back to me, she explained, "They're in a cabana behind us. I didn't exactly think that telling you we were being watched—not too closely—was conducive to a first date or whatever this is."

Chapter Thirteen

Lena

"I understand if you'd rather not spend a week with me," I said.

CJ's hands came to my shoulders. "I want to spend the week with you. I was just thrown off by the idea that they're watching you—us. That you need to be watched. Were they at breakfast?"

I nodded. "And at the pool yesterday."

His turquoise stare narrowed. "Are you in danger? Is that why the couple in the bushes startled you?"

I sat on the edge of the mattress and stared out at the sparkling water. Exhaling, I leaned down, resting my elbows on my legs. I couldn't explain my desire to share with CJ. It was out of character, but the truth was I rarely conversed with anyone outside of business. There was something settling and comforting in sharing, even a little. "I've had security for years. Without going into much detail, I travel a lot, and I'm a woman."

CJ crouched down on the sand near my feet. As his eyes met mine, he laid his hand on my knee. "Yes, Lena. I've noticed you're a woman."

"Lately, the threat has been more overt." I sat straighter, covering his hand with mine. For only a moment, I debated the degree to my sharing. It was odd that I was willing to share my body, but not my secrets. The secrets seemed more personal.

"Lena?"

"Someone is stalking me."

His jaw clenched and his brow furrowed. "Stalking you?"

For the next few minutes, I gave CJ the abbreviated version of the last few months—the break-in, the fish, then the fish arriving or showing up, and lastly, the candy.

"Jesus, Lena. Are the police involved?"

"Not at first, I didn't want the attention. With the candy, yes. That's why I'm here. My partner—business partner," I clarified, "and Adam, well everyone who works with me, thought I should leave town for a while. I haven't taken a week away from work for as long as I can remember. I guess you could say I'm hiding out."

CJ stood, brushed the sand from his knees, and sat

beside me. Taking my hand in his, he lifted it to his lips and kissed my palm. "I want to spend the week with you."

"I'm not prey." As I leaned my head against his solid shoulder, I tried to convince myself. Maybe if I denied it enough times, then just maybe I'd start to believe it again.

"You're not." He squeezed my hand. "You, Lena, are a hunter. A lioness."

I sat taller. "I know we don't really know each other, but I feel the need to tell you that who you see isn't me, not *the* Lena. When the break-in happened, when my fish were killed, it empowered me. Without details, I've come back from far worse. So when it happened, I was angry, livid at the violation. I was determined not to allow this man or woman, this person, to interrupt my life." My shoulders slumped. "The candy was different. It was an attempt on my life. Someone wants me dead. That's hard to ignore. It's gotten into my head and now..." I wasn't sure what now was.

CJ wrapped his arm around me. "You're safe with me."

I wanted to believe that.

"I'm glad you didn't eat it," CJ said, "but what alarmed you about the candy?"

"The note read as if it were a gift from my sister."

"Your sister tried to kill you?"

Not me, but I wasn't ready to share that family secret.

"No," I replied. "I knew it wasn't from her. It was postmarked in Missoula."

"The city where you live," he said.

I nodded. "They didn't sign her name but implied it was her. My sister is in Wisconsin. It felt off. Adam inspected the chocolate pieces and discovered pinpricks in the bottom. They were small, but he decided they should be inspected." I shrugged. "He was right."

CJ reached for my chin and turned my face toward his gaze. The turquoise swirled with emotion as he dropped his forehead to mine. "I'm sorry you're dealing with this. I'd like to take your mind off real life, if for only the rest of this week."

I forced a smile. "We were off to a pretty good start."

"Until our champagne bottle was mistaken for a gunshot."

"It was loud."

CJ stood and walked back to the ice bucket. "Take off the cover-up, scoot back on the bed, and let me bring you a glass of champagne."

The Lena didn't follow orders well. She gave them and expected them to be followed. And yet, without objection, I did as he'd said. With my hat, bag, and cover-up on the straw mat, I settled back on the inclined bed. Although I had an unimpeded view of the sparkling waters of the Caribbean, my focus was on the man closer.

Wearing only his swim trunks, I ogled at not only his physical attractiveness but at his genuine concern. I recognized it for the rarity that it was. Coming around the mattress, CJ held both glasses, extending one to me. Taking the glass, I said, "It's okay to admit that I'm too much trouble."

CJ sat on the edge of the mattress. The warmth of his bent leg radiated to mine as he lifted the glass. "So much trouble. Here's to finding out how much trouble you can be."

We both took a sip of the bubbly champagne.

"What do you want to do this week?"

I twisted the stem of the glass between my fingers. "Hiding out is new to me. My kindle is filled with books that I've been putting off for years." Squinting my eyes, I looked out at the water. "And this beach is beautiful."

CJ walked around to the other side of the mattress, refilled his glass, and sat at my side. "I'm inexperienced at hiding out. I'm also unaccustomed to free time." His smile shone my direction. "We can figure this out together."

As he secured my hand in his, I marveled at how much I enjoyed being close to him. It was different, yet strangely comforting. For an indeterminate amount of time, we sat, both silently watching the waves.

The alarm bells that were ringing earlier today on our walk had fallen silent. I wasn't sure if they were gone or only muffled by the presence of this man. Either way, for the first time since the candy arrived, I felt truly at peace.

I placed my empty glass on the straw mat and wrapping my arm around his, laid my head on his shoulder. My eyelids grew heavy as the curtains fluttered in the breeze. Napping in the middle of the day was also a rarity for me. I blamed the earlier mimosas and the recent champagne. It could be the sense of safety. Whatever it was, it was the perfect combination as I fell asleep.

When I woke, it took me a second to realize where I was. Shaking my head, I sat up, squinting at the brightness beyond the cabana. I was alone on the mattress, except for Kelsey who was sitting at the end.

"Kelsey?"

She turned my way with a grin. "You're awake."

"Where's CJ?"

"He went up to the pool to get you two lunch."

"And you saw him leave?" I asked.

"He came over to us."

"He did?"

She nodded. "He said he wasn't sure how this worked, but he didn't want to leave you alone. I came to you, and Adam went with CJ."

"He's with Adam? Did you two learn more about him?"

Kelsey nodded again as she took a drink of a water bottle. "No red flags."

I let out a breath. "Don't tell me more."

"There's an interesting connection, but nothing worrisome. Adam wanted to speak to him."

"No," I said, swinging my legs over the edge of the mattress. "I don't want Adam revealing anything about me. I've already shared more than I intended."

Kelsey stood. "Ms. Montgomery, Adam knows your rules. He also knows what he's doing. CJ will only learn about you from you."

Putting on my beach cover, I informed Kelsey that a walk up to the pool was in our future. As we walked together toward the resort, I asked, "What does your gut say about him?"

"Adam is incredibly competent."

I grinned. "CJ."

She smiled back at me. "My gut says that he's a good distraction for you. He's not the fish/candy person, and in over three years, I've never seen you take a nap. More often than not, you go to sleep after midnight and wake before five. My gut says that with everything going on, CJ is exactly what you need."

Chapter Fourteen

Lena

Present time

With Adam's hand in the small of my back, we hurried down an isolated stairwell. Our shoes clipped on the linoleum as my pulse raced in my ears. I leaned over the banister, wondering how many flights we had to go.

"Ms. Montgomery," Adam prodded. "We have a car waiting."

"This isn't real."

"It's a precaution."

"Tell me again what they said."

We were still moving lower and lower. With my purse hanging from my shoulder and Adam carrying my satchel with my laptop and notes, we'd made a quick departure from the meeting.

"They stopped a man in the lobby with a concealed firearm."

"That doesn't mean he was after me."

"Your name was on a letter they found in his pocket."

My name.

A seed of hope sprang to life as I stopped. "Wait, Adam, if this is the man, the fish and candy...if it's him, this is over."

"It's too early to make any assumptions. Right now, we're learning what we can and determining if he was working alone."

Nodding, I resumed our descent.

My questions kept coming. "What's his name?"

"I'm sure they'll find out." Adam turned his light-blue stare on me. "Right now, our priority is getting you away from this building."

"How did he know I was here? There's nothing public about Montgomery Holdings working with the gallery. Hell, we weren't even at the gallery but at their attorney's office in the middle of one of the biggest cities in the country. How did he know I was here?"

My mind swirled with thoughts of each person

involved in this deal. One of them said something. With each flight my anger grew.

Finally, we came to the ground floor.

Adam took his phone from the pocket inside his suit coat and sent a text.

We both looked up at the sound of footsteps coming from above.

"Come on," he said, wrapping his arm around my shoulder.

Beyond the door my senses were on overload. Hot sunshine streamed down as people pushed by one another. The sounds of traffic and the scent of exhaust infiltrated my senses. Adam pulled me closer, my shield if someone was waiting for us.

Someone was—the driver Adam had texted.

The dark sedan pulled up to the curb and within seconds I was in the back seat and Adam was in front with our driver. I let out a breath, realizing that my hands were cold and shaking.

Adam peered around the seat. "Are you good?"

"Good?" I scoffed, reaching for my own hand. "I've been better."

The driver looked from Adam to me. "Change of plans?"

"We're headed to the airport, Westchester."

The driver nodded as he merged the car into midday traffic.

My ears rang with the new silence as I tried to make sense of what had just happened. One minute I was going over the final proposal. The next, I was being rushed out of the office and down twenty-plus flights of stairs.

Taking my phone from my purse, I saw the picture I'd added as my background. For only a moment, I was back in Cancún with a smile on my face. That wasn't real life. Sighing, I closed my eyes. This was now my real life.

The driver was from a car service.

As we made our way onto 9A, I sent a text to Jeremy, hoping if I stayed busy, my trembling would stop.

"I'll call once I'm on the plane. Change of plans. I'm headed home."

My next text was to the attorney representing the gallery.

"I'll review the proposal and if everything is as we discussed, we'll send the signed contract by morning. Please advise Mr. Mueller this will not affect our agreement."

The attorney replied first.

"Ms. Montgomery, our sincerest apologies."

I replied.

"On the contrary. Hats off to your building's security."

Still holding my phone, I leaned back against the seat as my thoughts filled with the same questions from the stairwell. Narrowing my eyes, I looked up at the driver. He was the same one who picked us up at the airport yesterday and drove us to and from the Langham.

Had he told someone I'm here?

Who is the man with the gun? Is he my stalker or does he work for my stalker?

Nearly an hour after being whisked away from my meeting, we arrived at the Westchester County airport. The business jet belonged to Montgomery Holdings. The pilot and attendant were employed by me.

"Ms. Montgomery," Liz, the attendant, greeted as Adam and I walked toward the lowered steps.

Suddenly, I was suspicious of everyone, even trusted employees.

Nodding to Liz and the pilot Archie, I climbed the steps and made a right into the fuselage. As I sat down on a white leather seat and placed my purse on the chair beside me, I whispered to Adam.

"Are we sure of our employees?"

"No one gets near you who hasn't been thoroughly vetted."

Sighing, I buckled my seat belt and reached for my phone.

There were four texts and a missed call from Jeremy.

Hitting the icon, I returned his call.

"Holy shit, Lena. I've heard the story," he said by way of a greeting.

"You probably know more than I do." My gaze met Adam's. "I assume I'll hear more now that we're on the plane."

"I don't know much. The man's name is Bret or Brad. He's got a record. The guy is a burnt-out Ivy League trust-fund junkie."

"What's my connection to him?"

"Honey," Jeremy said, "his only connection was the five grand he was going to make by scaring you. He's denying that he would have shot you."

My eyes burned as tears came to the surface. I sucked in a breath. "That means this isn't over."

"They're going to find out who hired him."

Sniffing, I nodded. "This is so fucked up."

The plane began to move.

"Get home. You know Kelsey will make sure your place is safe."

Since we returned from Cancún, Kelsey had been staying at my house. She did her best to give me space. There was a pool house on the property, but she stayed in the main house. It was the fact I needed her that was bothering me more than the lack of privacy. Knowing my home had been broken into once still filled me with concern.

"I'll see you tomorrow morning."

"Remember, I'm headed to Austin. You need to get me that list."

List.

The list of Architech employees.

"Maybe I'll go with you," I suggested.

"You would be impressed to meet the Thompsons."

Lowering my elbow to the armrest, I nodded. "I'll be impressed when this nightmare is over."

"I'm making a day trip. I'll send Kelsey the information, and she can arrange everything for you and Adam. Change of scenery. And you'll be able to keep your mind busy with the list you're going to give me."

"The list. Yep, that's what I'll do after I have a couple fingers of bourbon."

"Love you," he said.

"Back at you."

No, Jeremy and I were not more than friends and associates. That didn't mean we hadn't enjoyed one another's company a time or two. The truth was that in my heart of hearts, I gravitated toward male companionship.

Jeremy did too.

What Jeremy and I loved the most about one another was that as a team, we complemented one another's skill set. He could find information on anyone or anything. He knew the financial forecasts, had the ability to see trends, and had an uncanny ability to find opportunities. As a Black man, he'd witnessed his share of inequalities present in the world we dominated. While my inequality was gender based, we worked well together.

While I'd been the one who first discovered Architech, Jeremy had been the one to work the acquisition. The roles were often reversed. With the stalker thing, my mind wasn't on Architech, and I knew Jeremy would succeed.

"Ma'am?" Liv said, "Would you like anything? We have a salad or sandwich for lunch. Iced tea?"

"Two fingers Black Label neat and a club salad."

"Mr. Dillon?"

"I'll have the sandwich and the iced tea." Adam looked at me with a slight grin. "Ms. Montgomery will have an iced tea also."

Though I flashed Adam a questioning stare, I nodded to Liz.

"You work for me," I said after she was gone.

"I do. Jeremy's been after you for a week to get that list done. The last time you started drinking at breakfast, you fell asleep."

Inhaling, I stretched my neck, thinking about the cabana, the sand, the ocean...CJ. "This isn't breakfast." I looked at my watch. "It's after noon. And considering our earlier excitement, I deserve a triple." I went on to tell Adam what Jeremy had said about the wannabe shooter. "Do you know any more information?"

Adam looked down at his phone. "Bret Phillips. He's known for petty crimes. It seems he was in a ski accident in college. Once he met oxycodone, they developed a close relationship. He's been in and out of rehab. All they've gotten so far is that he needed the money, so he agreed to this job. He said he wasn't supposed to shoot you, only scare you."

"Ms. Montgomery." Liz handed me my bourbon.

"Thank you, Liz."

After placing two iced teas on the table between us, she added, "I'll have your meals shortly."

Lifting the tumbler to my lips, I took a hefty sip. The amber liquor burned my tongue and throat before warming my circulation.

I set the glass on the table. "He succeeded."

"He didn't get close to you."

"He scared me. I'm going with Jeremy to Austin tomorrow."

For a brief second, I recalled CJ saying that Austin was where he currently called home. Of course, over two million other people did also. And there was the parting of ways—back to real life.

"It's short notice, but we'll get Montgomery security on it," Adam said.

"Jeremy said he would call Kelsey, but I know between the two of you, you'll get it worked out."

"You can take her if you want. I'm going too."

The bourbon must be working as I felt my cheeks rise. "This employee thing means I tell you."

"Right, you did. I'm going."

Taking a deep breath and letting it out, I looked over at my satchel on the seat beside Adam. "Hand me that. After lunch, I'll look at the bios. Do you have any idea how many employees Architech employed?"

"That hasn't exactly been on my radar."

I rolled my eyes. "Mine either. I guess that's about to change."

Chapter Fifteen

Lena

"I emailed you the list," I said to Jeremy as we walked together toward the Montgomery Holdings business jet. The sun had yet to rise. Nevertheless, in my standard skirt, blouse, blazer, and high-heels, I was ready to embrace *the* Lena Montgomery. In full disclosure, I was also prepared to get away, if only for a day.

The volume of Jeremy's deep baritone voice increased in volume due to the roar of nearby engines. "I looked at it briefly this morning, but I'm going to study it more on the plane. There was one name missing."

My volume also rose to the point I was nearly shouting. "You told me to make the list. If you wanted a say in it, you could have made it and saved me the time."

Jeremy lifted his hands with a grin before motioning for me to go up the steps into the plane. It was the same plane I flew in from New York less than fifteen hours ago. It was the plane I and others in my company regularly used. The only time I hadn't was to my hideout week.

Enough about that. This was real life.

Simply stepping into the fuselage lowered the extraneous noise.

"Ms. Montgomery, Mr. Wilde," Liz said with her ever-present smile.

I simply nodded, more interested in Jeremy's and my conversation than Liz's greeting. Adam and Kelsey were a step behind us. Leading the way, I went back to the second set of seats and placing my purse in the seat to my side, sat. Jeremy took the seat opposite mine. The placement of the bag was a not-so-subtle hint that Adam and Kelsey were welcome to sit elsewhere.

After taking off his suit coat, Jeremy buckled his seat belt, and continued speaking. "Hear me out. Chandler Thompson truly wants to continue working with Architech."

"It's not Architech any longer, not the one he helped create. It's a Venus subsidiary, a Montgomery subsidiary. We paid over two hundred million for their technology. The last thing we need is a leech hanging on and possibly causing upheaval with the other retained employees."

Jeremy's lips were pressed in a straight line. His dark orbs were on me. I'd seen this look before. He had a point to make and he planned to do so. There was no doubt I'd managed to surround myself with handsome men even if they were mostly off-limits.

Today Jeremy's dark hair was plaited in tight braids giving him a professional appearance. It worked for him. While Kelsey might have been right that Jeremy could rock the surfing cat shirt, I admired the way he filled out his blue suit even without the jacket and tie.

"I'm glad you're along on this trip," he said. "You can be the one to tell Chandler."

I shrugged and narrowed my gaze. "Surely you know me better than that. Firing people doesn't lose me any sleep. Hell, this isn't even firing. It's not retaining."

Jeremy shook his head. "All I can say is I've met the guy on more than one occasion. He's smart. He created the technology that is already making us money. He has a lot to offer, and I don't get the sense that he has nefarious motives. I think the guy genuinely wants to stay on."

"Then why sell?"

"Two hundred and twenty million reasons."

"Take the money and run."

Jeremy narrowed his gaze. "When you and I met, we were younger, but we had similar drives."

I nodded, wondering why we were taking a walk down memory lane.

"Did you stop at your first million?"

"We paid a lot more than one million."

"My point is," he said, "Chandler shares our drive. His brother" —Jeremy shrugged— "not so much. Colton is a nice guy, but I get the feeling he's content with the dollar signs."

"Chandler isn't," I said. "Fine. He can use his windfall to create a never-dreamed-of new technology or turn it into a billion. I don't care." I took my laptop out of my bag, placing it on the table. "We can discuss this situation more."

Liz appeared at our side. "Archie is about to take off. He said it will be three and a half hours from wheels up to wheels down."

I glanced at my watch. Nothing that waking before four in the morning won't accomplish. With the time difference we'd arrive before eleven o'clock in Austin. Jeremy had the meeting set with the employees for one.

Before that we were scheduled to meet with the Thompson brothers. "Thank you, Liz."

"Would the two of you like anything before we take off?"

"Coffee," Jeremy and I said in unison.

Once she was gone, he smiled. "Caffeine type of morning."

Opening my eyes with a sigh, I rubbed my forehead and nodded. "Can we agree that there are less expensive cities to locate Architech?"

Jeremy nodded. "I've informed Colton that we're currently looking at space in a few different states. I've got people looking into the tax breaks and ramifications."

"Good," I said.

Jeremy's voice dropped to a whisper. "Girl, how are you holding up?"

"With duct tape and chicken wire, but I don't have any other choice."

"Anything new on the handwriting?"

I shook my head.

His gaze shimmered. "You need another week in paradise with that sexy man."

My cheeks rose as my lips curled into a smile. "I never said he was sexy."

"You didn't have to. I heard it in your voice every time I called."

"Yeah, well, that wasn't real life. This is."

By the time the plane left the ground, we both had our laptops booted up and cups of coffee before us.

"Willingness to relocate is a consideration for retention. I also looked at overlap," I began. "Under the Montgomery Holdings umbrella, we don't need two identical departments. It creates chaos and confusion."

For the next nearly two hours, we went through each of Architech's forty-two employees as well as the two previous owners.

Jeremy said, "I planned meeting with the Thompsons first and then addressing the employees as a whole. Once that's done, any individual employee who wants to speak to me may. I've had the severance packages worked out for over a week. Now with this list, Gigi is getting the right package assigned to the right employee. Again, nothing is settled until each employee agrees. Our HR team has been on this for a week on the ground in Austin, working out the preliminaries."

I looked over at my friend. "I'm sorry it's taken so long for me to get this list worked out. My mind..."

Jeremy reached across the table, turning his hand

palm up. With a grin, I took his hand as his grasp surrounded mine.

"Lena, this will end, and you know those two people behind me would never let anything happen to you."

"I know." I exhaled. "It's the randomness that's getting to me. Nothing happens for two or three weeks, then in one day two fish are found. Add to that, the candy and hell, the guy with the gun... No one should have known I was there. My house, fine—not fine, but you know what I mean."

"It's exhausting. I get it."

Nodding, I briefly closed my eyes and inhaled.

"Any news on Madison?" Jeremy asked.

I looked around for Liz. When I caught her eye, I lifted my coffee cup. Her nod meant she would arrive with a refill. Turning back to Jeremy, I answered. "It's looking good that Wisconsin will lower her charge to a class F felony. The psychiatric reports put her capable of going to court, but not of taking care of herself. They're concerned that she could be a danger to herself or others if rightly provoked. If they change the charge, she can agree to mandated treatment at a secure facility."

"Have Donovan or Julia chimed in?"

I shook my head. "No, they support me supporting

Madison. Van said he'd drop all charges, but he can't. It's the state vs. Madison Thomas."

Jeremy sat back and crossed his arms over his chest. "Do you ever feel like screaming?"

Warmth filled my cheeks as I grinned. "I did a few times in paradise."

"Details please." He looked at his watch. "We have over an hour before we get to Austin and a three-and-a-half-hour flight home. Come on, spill."

I shook my head. "I want to keep it."

He lifted his eyebrows. "Close to the heart."

"It's nothing and something. I blocked his number." Sighing, I looked at my friend. "Firing people is easier than that was. Telling this Chandler guy to go on with his life will be a cakewalk." I shrugged. "I couldn't say goodbye to CJ, not again."

"He got to you."

Liz appeared with the coffee pot. "Would you like breakfast before we land?"

A peek out the side window told me that the sun was up, and the day had started.

"Yes," I replied. "Fruit, yogurt, and granola."

Liz nodded and turned to Jeremy. After he ordered a breakfast sandwich, Liz walked away.

"He got to you," Jeremy repeated.

"It's that I'm in a weird place with everything

happening. I guess I could say it was refreshing to let my guard down. I can't do that in real life. I can't do that today in the meetings. The impenetrable walls keep me detached."

"You've let me in."

I smiled. "You're different."

"Speaking of the Shermans, did I tell you that Donovan called while you were away?"

"Don't tell me that he heard I was gone and wanted to invoke his right to temporarily run Montgomery."

Jeremy smiled. "He called about Architech. Wanted the details."

"Sorry, Van. I beat you to this one."

"That's what he said. He also offered to double whatever I make with you to start working for him." Jeremy furrowed his brow. "I think he could have been serious."

"You can't leave me."

"No worries. I told him that no number of zeros could get me to leave."

I sat taller. "See, if Chandler Thompson didn't want to sell, the same would be true. He sold. It's time for him to go."

"No one knows the technology like he does."

"You really want to retain him?" I asked.

"My gut tells me it would be the smartest move. What if something goes wrong or needs to be tweaked? Chandler knows all the ins and outs. You yourself said this technology is a gold mine. The purchase price will be made up in profits, but not if we can't manage what we have."

"Surely someone else—"

Jeremy shook his head. "I gave you the bios. There are some excellent employees, but the nuts and bolts, that has always been the Thompson brothers. I think we'd be foolish to turn down this opportunity."

Chapter Sixteen

Chandler

"I'm not a fan of suits," I said to Colton as I tugged on the sleeve of the suit coat. Together we were standing in what used to be his office at what was Architech, the company we'd created from the ground up. The company name and everything else about it was no longer our decision.

When I turned my brother's direction, the empty bookcases and lack of furniture hit me like a punch in the gut. "Hard to believe that after today we may never step foot back in this building."

Colton nodded. "It sounds as if Venus is planning a move, a physical move—out of Austin. Out of Texas. They're inquiring and have the possibilities down to three or four cities, all in different states. I've talked to some of the people out there" —he tilted his head toward the door— "and most people are willing to make the move to stay with Architech."

"I'm willing," I admitted. "Talking to Jeremy over the last few weeks, I felt pretty good about the ability to stay on, but now...now that it's the day, I'm getting a bad vibe."

"Listen to me. It feels good, cutting the cord. Just think, you could spend more amazing weeks in Cancún."

I scoffed. "It wasn't the place that made the week fantastic."

"Have you called her?"

"The way the call drops, I think she blocked my number."

Colton's eyes opened wide. "Oh fuck. I'm sorry."

Leaning against the wall, I crossed my arms over my chest. "Maybe I'm stupid, but I don't think she blocked me because she doesn't like me, but because she does. At least that's what I'm holding onto. We agreed on one week. Worst agreement ever made."

"Worse than selling Architech, that's big."

"I'm staying with Venus, barring a restraining order."

Colton laughed. "Yeah, you can be tenacious." His expression sobered. "You'll meet that special someone. Give it time."

I thought I had. I didn't go to Cancún to meet my forever, but now that time has passed without Lena's smile and laugh, without waking up with her sexy body at my side, I realized that she was someone special, maybe not mine but definitely special.

"Maybe that someone is in a new city," I said, "wherever Venus takes Architech."

The door to the office opened as Peter, our top assistant, peered inside. "Jeremy Wilde just called. Their plane has landed."

The coffee in my gut churned as my gaze went from Peter to my brother. "It's showtime."

"He also said," Peter added, "that the owner of Venus is with him, a Ms. Montgomery."

Colton stood taller as he inhaled. "Big guns."

Peter nodded. "The conference room is ready for the four of you as soon as they arrive, and everyone will be present in the break room by 12:50 p.m."

That was the largest room in this building for Jeremy, or this Ms. Montgomery, to address all the employees.

After the door closed and Peter left, Colton turned toward me. "Man, you look like someone just stole your dog. Snap out of it. The money is ours, and the future is up to them. Pass the baton and all that shit."

Reins.

A memory flashed in my mind.

Colton continued, "We did our part by negotiating for our people."

I eyed him up and down. He too was dressed to impress, not our usual attire. "Then tell me again why we're dressed up for a funeral."

"I'm sending you back to Cancún. Your negativity is getting on my nerves."

"Your positivity is getting on mine."

We both started to laugh. This was who we were, brothers, friends, and enemies.

"I don't want you to move away," Colton said. "Neither does Devon."

"You can visit anytime. Get your own jet."

"It's been a great ride, CJ. I mean that." He looked around the room. "The Thompson boys made it big." His arm went around my neck. "Couldn't ask for a better kid brother."

"Me moving with Venus, wherever they send Architech, isn't about leaving you or Devon."

"I know that. I want you to know we'll miss you."

After a few pats on the back, we both stood tall.

I was barely an inch taller than Colton. He had the same color hair, but his was shorter, and his eyes were greener than mine. Two years my senior meant that he was only thirty-three.

"We broke the mold," I said. "Mom and Dad are proud."

"Paid off Mom and Dad's house like we agreed."

I grinned. "That's good news. Do they know?"

"Not yet. I can't wait for that phone call."

My brother was right. "It has been a wild ride. I'm not ready to get off."

"To the conference room?" he asked.

"Yeah, but first, let's take a walk around the facility. If their plane just landed, the traffic will take them a while to get here."

While our office suites were virtually bare, the rest of the facility was still operating—that was until Venus decided it was time to move locations. Together we made our way down to the different departments, peering through windows as employees continued to work. The hard soles of our shoes clipped along the tile.

"We'll miss you," Harrison, a man in our quality-control department, said as we passed in the hallway.

"Venus has made some promises."

"We know you two have done your best regarding us," he said. "We also acknowledge we would have done the same thing. Life is what it is. I'll go on to wherever they take Architech, or if they don't want me, I won't."

As we walked beyond Harrison, I let out a sigh of relief. "I hope that sentiment isn't the exception. It would make me feel less shitty."

"Devon keeps reminding me that we did our part for the employees. We need faith that the promises Jeremy made will come to pass. The attorneys crossed the T's and dotted the I's."

"I'm wondering about this Montgomery lady," I said. "Why would she show up here and not in any of the negotiations?"

Colton shook his head as he opened the door to the conference room. "I don't know. This whole having money thing is new. Maybe she wanted to see what she bought."

"Buyer's remorse."

"Too late for that."

The room was set with a water pitcher and glasses upon a long glass table. The window at the far end looked out onto Austin's skyline, well, part of it. Our facility was only three stories tall, and this room as well as our offices were on the top floor.

"Or," I suggested as we took our seats on the far side of the table, "she's here to pull a bait and switch."

"Do you think we should have invited the attorneys?" Colton asked.

"Shit, man, the deal is done. The grace period expired. I guess we need to be ready for anything."

At about five until twelve, Peter opened the conference room door and extended his arm toward us. "Mr. Colton Thompson and Mr. Chandler Thompson."

We stood as the door opened wider. There were more than two people. Seeing the familiar faces, I almost didn't hear the rest of Peter's announcement.

"Ms. Lena Montgomery and Mr. Jeremy Wilde are here."

Lena?

The most beautiful chocolate gaze fixed on mine as my mouth went dry and my heart forgot to beat.

Chapter Seventeen

CJ

Three weeks ago

The balcony bar was quieter than the pool during this time in the afternoon. Sitting at a table near the railing, Lena and I sipped our drinks while simmering in the Mexico sunshine. The umbrella over our table cast its shadow to our side. There was another tiny one in Lena's drink.

"I was thinking we could have dinner brought to my suite," I said, looking across the table at Lena. With the last two days of sun, her skin had a bronze glow contrasting her white sundress. Large golden earrings hung from her ears and many golden bracelets jingled from her wrist. However, my attention was on the way her pink lips curled into a smile and the way her top foot swung with her legs crossed.

Since yesterday, she seemed more relaxed.

If I could do anything to facilitate that, I would.

"Adam or Kelsey will have to check your suite."

I nodded. "Adam told me."

"What else did he tell you?"

"All your deep, dark secrets."

She turned toward the ocean and lifted her chin. From this angle I could see beneath her sunglasses as she grinned. "Well, then I guess it's settled." She turned back. "He's fired."

"That means I have to spend the rest of this week with you and Kelsey." I shrugged. "I've had worse vacations."

"I can't believe you're wearing that shirt," she said with a giggle.

I looked down at the surfing cat. Instead of a surfboard, the cat was surfing on a piece of pizza. When I looked up, Lena had her straw between her lips, drinking a frozen daiquiri. My first thought was her offer yesterday to relieve my big issue. The whole popping-champagne-cork incident took us a different direction.

"Where did you even get it?"

"The shirt?" I questioned. "Oh, you see, it's a valuable family heirloom passed down for generations." When she only shook her head, I added, "I recall you saying that you didn't care if I wore clothes."

"I don't think those were my exact words, but you're right. Now, I admit the statement was too broad. How could I have ever predicted your interesting fashion sense?"

"Interesting?"

"Unique."

"I can go back to the shop where I found yesterday's shirt, but I think you should know, the cashier is hot for me."

Lena nodded as she pressed her lips together. "There's no ring on your finger. Maybe this cashier has a thing for cats and you'll get lucky."

I leaned slightly toward her over the table and lowered my timbre. "I don't need a ring to know who I want to spend time with, clothed or unclothed."

"Come to my suite for dinner," she suggested.

"Do I need a code word to get past your security?"

Her cheeks pinkened. "Maybe a safe word for once you're inside."

Trying to swallow, I almost choked on my seltzer.

Lena's smile turned to a full laugh. Her hands came to her cheeks. "Tell me I'm not blushing."

"You're blushing."

"I don't blush."

"It appears you do." I sat back against the chair and crossed my arms over my chest. "Walrus."

"Walrus?"

"My safe word."

Lena's slender eyebrows rose above her sunglasses. "Is that your standard safe word or a random thought?"

"I have a whole list."

She nodded. "Interesting."

"Yeah, but the thing is, I offer the list when a woman can't come up with her own. It saves time. Sometimes going over the contract gets laborious."

"I agree, you have to watch the fine print."

I had very little clue what I was talking about, other than what I learned from a movie I made the mistake of watching with my mother. Nevertheless, I remembered a few things.

"Are you saying I'll need a safe word?" Lena asked with her eyebrows again raised.

Reaching across the table, our fingers met until they were intertwined. "I'll share."

She looked to where our hands were connected and back. "Sharing is good. As for entry, no, I'll tell them that you're coming."

"We could tell them now."

"I was thinking seven o'clock. The sunset is at seven thirty. We can have room service."

"I'll bring dinner. You're supplying the atmosphere. Is there anything I should know, allergies, likes, dislikes...?"

"It seems that Adam didn't fully fill you in." When I only shook my head, Lena placed a finger on her chin, appearing to be in deep thought. "No allergies, except to sulfa medications. Dislikes would include chocolate candy with pinpricks."

That was a subject I wanted to avoid. "Now tell me likes."

She looked at my shirt and smiled. "Pizza."

"Veggie, no cheese."

Lena shook her head, the tips of her deep red hair swinging near her chin. "I love cheese. While admittedly, I don't indulge in pizza often, when I do, the greasier the better. Thin crust, pepperoni." She grinned. "I know from yesterday's and today's breakfasts that you don't shy away from meat."

"Carnivore, remember." I imagined the delicacy she described. "My brother and I went on a business trip to New York, and there was a shop near our hotel. I swear it was always open. We'd go down late at night. They sold it—"

"By the slice," she said, completing my sentence. "That's the best."

"Then that's my quest for today, to find us the best New-York-style pizza in Cancún."

Her smile dimmed. "Don't leave the resort."

"There is no journey I won't make for this pizza. If I have to fly to New York and back, I will have our feast."

"I hope you don't disappoint me."

"Never."

"Do you and your brother work together?"

I tilted my head. "Real life."

"You said you went together on a business trip." She waved her hand, her bracelets jingling. "No, you're right. Here and now."

"We did. Not anymore."

Lena leaned back and stared at me. Even though her eyes were covered by the dark sunglasses, I felt her gaze upon me.

"I'm sorry," she said. "That makes you sad."

"You make me happy. That real life will be around next week. You won't." When she didn't reply, I asked, "What are you thinking?"

"This week versus next. Kelsey said she approved of you. She said that you're a good distraction."

"Is that what I am?"

"You've distracted me," Lena said. "What am I?"

"A lioness."

"To you?"

"A beautiful distraction. Since talking to you the other afternoon at the bar, I've been blissfully distracted from real life. You know, that thing we've sworn not to discuss? You appearing on the treadmill at my side was a gift from the gods. I look forward to more distracting."

"I recognized you."

"In the gym?"

She nodded. "I'm glad I chose that treadmill."

"Me too."

As Lena stood, the neckline of the dress lowered, giving me only a hint at the tits I'd had on display yesterday afternoon. Pulling my gaze away from her curves, I also stood and reached for her hands.

The sandals she wore were flat. I stood easily seven or eight inches taller than her. "Are you leaving me?"

"I'm going up to my suite. I want to give you time to hunt for our dinner."

"I'll miss you."

"Seven o'clock," she said, her fingers slipping from my grasp as she stepped away.

I took a step toward her. "How about a kiss?"

She shook her head with a grin. "I'm holding them

hostage, my insurance policy that you won't stand me up and more importantly, leave me hungry."

"I will collect. Suite number?"

"I'll text you."

We'd exchanged numbers sometime yesterday. I'd gone to sleep with her text. I had hope that tonight, instead of holding my phone, I would be holding her.

Lena's light-brown gaze stayed on me for a moment until she turned and walked toward the steps that led to one of the many pools. Watching from afar, I waited until I saw Kelsey approach Lena.

Relief flooded my circulation, knowing that Lena was in safe hands.

Tonight, I wanted those hands to be mine.

Removing my phone from my pocket, I began my hunt.

Chapter Eighteen

Lena

"Creed Royal Service," Kelsey said as she entered my suite.

"A smidgen."

After leaving CJ, I'd gone to one of the resort shops and purchased two bottles of wine and the green sundress I was now wearing. Next, I'd returned to my suite, showered, and shaved. If yesterday afternoon was a prelude to tonight, I wanted to be better prepared. Now my hair was done, I wore a bit more makeup, and the atmosphere was set.

"It's overkill. Isn't it?" I asked as Kelsey looked around the living room of my suite illuminated with candles—lots of candles.

"No, I'm sure CJ won't take off running over a fire hazard."

"Maybe he's a fireman?" I shrugged. "I mean, he could be. He looks the part—hot and buff."

"Do you want to know his profession?"

I shook my head. "No. That's real life." Turning toward the open door to the balcony, I recalled what CJ had said about his brother. "He seemed sad when he mentioned that he and his brother no longer worked together." I spun back to Kelsey. "I hope his brother didn't die in a fire." My eyes opened wide. "Yeah, the candles are a bad idea."

Kelsey began to laugh. "This is so not you, and I have to admit, it's entertaining."

My fists went to my hips. "What's not me?"

"In a matter of seconds, you created an entire backstory on a man you barely know. A tragic backstory."

"Am I warm?"

"Are we now playing that game where one person is supposed to answer either warmer or cooler?"

"I don't know." I looked out at the pink and orange sky. "I've never dated anyone or even had a one-night stand with someone who I've known so little about." I grinned as I turned back to Kelsey. "See, old dog, new tricks."

"You aren't old."

"I'm not, you're right. I'm also not young, and

while I don't know by how much, I'm certain CJ is younger. Did you see that shirt?"

Kelsey scoffed. "I think that shirt is an example of CJ's confidence, whatever his age. I mean, Adam wouldn't wear that shirt and he's a confident man." She grinned. "Jeremy might."

As I blew out some of the candles, Kelsey asked, "Do you need anything else for tonight?"

I looked at my watch. It was almost seven. "Just CJ and pizza."

"We're across the hall if you need anything. The camera is set on your door."

Real life.

"Is there any reason to believe the fish stalker knows we're here?"

"No, ma'am."

I let out a breath. "Have you or Adam heard from the Montgomery security or Missoula police regarding the candy?"

"The only fingerprints were ours—yours, Adam's, and mine. The person was extremely careful. They're still working on the note."

A chill ran through me. Wrapping my arms around my midsection, I told myself to live in the here and now. That was the point of distractions. They were supposed to distract me.

"Don't think about it," Kelsey said as the entry door to the suite opened.

We both turned as CJ and Adam entered.

It wasn't only the box in CJ's hand that made me smile. It was the way he was looking at me, the curve of his grin, the presence of his dimple, the dampness of his untethered dark hair, and his white shirt. The surfing cat was gone. As my scan concluded at his canvas loafers, I realized he wasn't wearing a bathing suit.

With my feet bare, I made my way across the room and offered to take the box, the delicious aroma already had my stomach growling.

With a grin, CJ held the box tight. "No pizza until I get my kiss."

Putting my hands on his shoulder, I lifted myself up on my tiptoes until our lips touched. Soft and sweet, our connection was chaste. My attention went to our audience. "Thank you. I know you're close."

Adam and Kelsey nodded.

"Have a nice evening," Kelsey said as they both disappeared behind the double doors.

Quickly, I secured the deadbolt and turned back to CJ. "I'm sure you think that's weird."

"I feel like I'm in high school and they're your parents."

I scoffed. "We're not in high school and technically, they work for me. I'm their boss. And as I told you, Kelsey approves."

"Adam?"

"He doesn't chime in on my intimate relationships."

"Intimate," CJ said with a grin.

Setting the pizza box on the large table before the sofa, CJ came my way. Flames flickered and roared to life in his turquoise stare. My feet were rooted to the floor as his powerful long legs moved with purpose, shortening the distance between us.

I may be the lioness, but at this moment, CJ was the lion, king of the beasts, and he was looking at me as if I was his next meal.

My nipples beaded as he framed my cheeks, pulling me to him, flattening my breasts as my soft met his hard. Meeting him with equal parts desire and attraction, our lips again united. Unlike moments earlier, there was nothing chaste in this kiss. Possessive and heated, our heads turned as our tongues danced. Breathing was overrated as his hands roamed down my arms and curves.

My hands explored too—the definition in his muscles, broad shoulders, and strong arms.

Step by step we moved, our connection unsevered

until my shoulders collided with the wall. Lifting my ass, CJ pressed against me. I wrapped my legs around his waist and my arms around his neck, holding on, yet knowing he wouldn't let me fall. The longer we kissed the more aware I was of the hardness at my core, the more desperate my desire became as I wiggled against him with need, wanting a connection with what our clothes were preventing.

"Lena, are you wet?"

"Yes."

Our words were breathy and barely audible.

He began bunching the hem of my dress as his fully blazing gaze met mine. "I want to find out for myself."

I nodded as I was lost in the blue flames within his orbs.

When I was only a girl, my mother told me that blue flames were safe, meaning you were protected. She would say that seeing a blue flame in a candle was a good sign. It meant your guardian angel was looking over you. After her death, I searched for the blue flame, and now, decades later, I saw it.

My breath caught as CJ's fingers found my core.

With my hands on his shoulders, our stare-off continued as he found a rhythm. My lips pursed as he added another finger, and his thumb circled my clit.

"Come on my hand."

I wanted that, more than I wanted anything else. "Don't stop."

Lowering his lips to my neck, he continued his ministrations. The scruff of his unshaved face tingled my sensitive skin.

My body bounced and my core contracted as the synapses exploded, setting off fireworks through my circulation. There was no stopping the overwhelming escalation in endorphins. Holding tighter to his shoulders, I collapsed in his arms.

Holy shit.

Kissing wasn't CJ's only talent.

When I lifted my face from his shoulder, I was met with his stunning smile.

"You're absolutely magnificent, Lena." He laid a kiss on my forehead as he gently released his hold, and my feet found the floor.

Still holding his shoulders, I prayed my wobbly knees wouldn't give out. Looking up at him, I smiled. "You are. That was..." I let my forehead drop to his solid chest. My question was muffled against his soft shirt. "Are you a fireman?"

His chest vibrated with his laugh.

I looked back up at his mesmerizing stare. "Is that funny?"

"It's random."

"Yeah." I shrugged. "You see I just had a fantastic orgasm, and well, words were failing me."

CJ lifted his fingers to his lips and sucked. "Fantastic? You taste fantastic."

Reaching for his hand, I opened my lips and slowly sucked his fingers, while swirling my tongue.

"Fuck, Lena."

Feeling this was too one-sided, I dropped to my knees and peered up at him. "My turn."

He reached for my chin. "We have pizza."

"I like cold pizza."

Chapter Nineteen

CJ

Lena was a vision, sitting back on her heels, staring up at me with those amazing light-chocolate orbs. "It's your turn to tell me to stop."

I would bite off my own tongue if it even considered taking her up on that offer.

Her lips curled as she sat forward, her fingers nimbly working the buttons on my shorts. When she discovered my lack of underwear, her smile widened. "I see you were prepared."

Her touch was tender and controlled with absolutely no hesitancy. She pushed my shorts down to my knees and with one last veiled glance my direction, held my cock and using one finger, wiped the come glistening at the tip. My heart beat in double time as she put her finger between her lips, as if she were tasting the icing on a penis-shaped cake.

A satisfied hum filled my ears seconds before she opened her lips.

Fuck.

My eyes rolled back as she took me deep, her fingers running the length of my shaft.

Pushing my shorts down, I stepped out of one leg, spreading my stance before reaching for the wall to keep myself upright. I couldn't recall being this hard. It was painful and sensational at the same time.

My knees locked and my thighs tensed as the pressure built.

"Jesus, Lena."

I was in the hands of a master, the way one hand now rolled my balls and the other hand worked in tandem with her exquisite mouth. It was as Lena swirled her tongue at the sensitive tip that I knew I wouldn't last much longer.

I tried to take a step back, but Lena wouldn't break our connection.

"Shit, I'm going to come."

My comment only increased her speed and conviction. Before I realized, I was rocking with her, her head in my hands. Everyone and everything else ceased to exist. Completely lost in the moment, the finale came much as an explosion of fireworks on a summer night. Releasing her head, I concentrated on standing. Lena didn't stop until I was cleaned.

"That was phenomenal."

She placed one last kiss on the still-erect cock and stood with a grin. Without a word, Lena reached for the hem of my shirt, and lifted it over my head. With a hum, she walked around me, circling me as her fingertips left a ghost of a touch and her gaze scanned every inch of me. On her second pass, I reached out, pulling her close.

"Do you approve of what you see?"

"Very much." She took a step back, looked at my cock and back to me. "It seems that didn't fully resolve the issue."

Lena was right. The way she was looking at me had me back to rock hard.

"Do you have any suggestions?" I asked.

Her chocolate eyes opened wide. "Wait, you didn't take a blue pill, did you? I mean do we need to start a timer. Over four hours requires medical attention."

Wrapping my arms around her, I lifted her up and spun her around. Her laughter filled the air. I lowered her feet to the floor, thinking how light she felt in my arms. And yet as petite as she was, there was nothing frail about this astonishing woman.

"I don't need a pill, and you can start the timer, but I guarantee if your bodyguards don't kick me out, I can last longer than four hours."

Her eyebrows danced. "That sounds like a challenge." She lifted my shorts from the floor and handed them my direction. "Would you like to dress for dinner?"

I slowly turned a circle, noticing that her suite was similar to mine. There was one difference. Out on her balcony was a private pool, not large, but easily big enough for two.

Shaking my head, I let the shorts drop to the floor and stepped closer, teasing the spaghetti straps of her green dress. "No, Lena. I want you to join me on the balcony, stark naked, to watch the sun set."

Her lips curled upward as soft pink filled her cheeks.

"Lose the dress."

"I just bought it."

"Then you probably don't want me to rip it off you."

"Hmm."

As she'd done to me moments ago, I circled her, looking for buttons or a zipper. There were none. Once I was again facing her, she crossed her arms, taking hold of the dress, and pulled it upward. I watched with bated breath as the hem rose higher, revealing her scant panties and to my utter delight, no bra.

When the dress joined my shorts and shirt, I took her in. "You're still overdressed."

Without hesitation, Lena pushed her panties down and stepped out.

"You are exquisite," I said, scanning her from head to toe.

She turned toward the balcony. "We're about to miss the sunset."

I reached for her hand and led her out onto the balcony. Before us was the water. Above, dusk fought with the daylight as vibrant colors filled the sky. We weren't visible to anyone from this height and still, I asked, "Is this too public?"

Lena shook her head. "Private indecency. My bucket list."

Holding her in front of me, we both watched as the sun met the horizon. "Did you hear it?"

She craned her neck back to me. "Hear what?"

"The sun. It sizzles when it touches the water."

Smiling, she shook her head and looked back at the water. "Some say there's a green flash when the sun fully submerges below the horizon. It's kind of like the aurora borealis, depending on the perfect atmospheric conditions—the sun interacting with the earth's magnetic field."

"Have you ever seen it?"

She shook her head.

With my arms around her, we stood in silence until the sun was gone. At that final second, I swore I saw what she described. "I think I saw it."

"That was beautiful," Lena said.

I spun her around again, circling her waist with my arms and tugging her flesh against mine. "You're beautiful." I looked down at the pool. "My suite doesn't have a pool."

"It's not very big."

"It's plenty big for the two of us."

She tilted her head. "I like the way you think."

"Let me get the pizza." As I started to pick it up, Lena carried a few candles out to the balcony. "I should have brought wine," I called out to her.

Her perfect silhouette appeared in the open doorway. "I have two bottles, white and red. I didn't know what you liked."

"Right now, it's both."

"I'll get the wine and glasses."

The pool water was warmer than I anticipated. An old episode of Seinfeld came back to me. Shrinkage shouldn't be a problem. I encouraged Lena to sit in front of me, between my legs, both of us facing the sea. As the warm breeze blew over us, Lena laid her head back against my chest.

Distraction.

I could be a distraction, and I could be distracted. If I gave that more thought, I'd admit that there was more I wanted. In two short days, I'd found this woman addicting. If she were a drug, I'd use my newfound fortune to buy a lifelong supply.

Sitting up, Lena reached for the two glasses of red wine and handed one to me. This time she settled facing me. "Thank you, CJ."

"I am most certain after what happened in there, I should be thanking you."

Hiding her grin behind the rim of the glass, Lena shook her head. "When I agreed to get away for a week, I chose here hoping that with the climate and security, I could take a break from real life. Honestly, I never thought it would happen. I'm pretty much a type-A personality. This week is the result of me losing control, and if it weren't for meeting you, I'd be like a caged animal in paradise. A lion in a zoo is still caged."

I took a drink of the red blend, pleased that it wasn't too sweet. "That's good." I lifted the glass toward her. "The only one who can cage you, Lena, is you. I hope this asshole is found and you can break free to be the predator you are. She's there. I sense her in you."

"I'm not prey."

"No, you're not."

As we spoke, the sky darkened, and stars began to appear above the endless water. I opened the pizza box to exactly what Lena had asked for. My quest wasn't an easy one. I found getting New-York-style pizza in this resort a challenge—I didn't back away from challenges. After offering a rather large tip to the chef of the Italian restaurant, I convinced him to prepare a special order, one not found on the menu.

Taking out a large triangular slice, I moved to Lena's side. "Open."

Her eyes sparkled. "I can feed myself."

"You can. I'm pampering you."

Her lips opened as I placed the end of the pizza in her mouth. After she bit down, I shook my head. "I'm glad you didn't bring out those teeth earlier."

For long enough to have our skin prune, we sat, ate, drank, talked, and kissed. A crescent moon hung over the sea. It was after the bottle was empty and the box had only the grease stain to hint at what it had contained that I offered Lena my hand. "I want a tour."

We both stood, the water dripping from our bodies. "Tour?"

"Of your suite."

She took my hand and stepped out of the pool. The candlelight flickered in the breeze, and the suite within was dark with only a few candles. With her in the lead, I followed into the living area. One by one she blew out the candles, her lips pert and her ass on display within the moonlight streaming through the glass. Searching my discarded shorts, I found the three packs of condoms.

"Three?" Lena said when I opened my palm.

"Four hours, remember."

Passing a small kitchen and the door to the bathroom, we continued through the darkness until we were both standing in the bedroom.

The only illumination came from the starry and moon-filled sky beyond another set of French doors. With her face tipped up to mine, I cupped her cheek. "I've wanted to be inside you since I saw you at the pool."

Lena nodded, her face rocking under my touch.

"You are not prey. You're fucking strong. I can't promise I'll be gentle."

"I don't want gentle, CJ. I want to forget everything except the here and now. I want to scream your name."

My erection was back to full staff.

"Walrus," I said as I led her to the bed.

She pushed me to the edge of the mattress. As I sat, Lena reached for one of the condoms and opened the wrapper. Slowly, she sheathed my cock, taking her time as I doubled in size under her touch. Climbing up on my lap with her hands on my shoulders, Lena straddled my legs and lowered herself.

My back arched as her body squeezed my erection.

Lena didn't stop until she had all of me. Her chocolate gaze met mine. "I hope I can walk tomorrow."

Holding her, I stood and spun, lowering her to the bed and following her so as to not break our connection. Her squeal filled the air. Pushing her knees up, I moved in and out. "You won't be able to if I can help it."

Chapter Twenty

Lena

Stretching, I opened my eyes, waking for the fourth and final morning with CJ. I could extend my stay, but real life had responsibilities. One was my sister. Her attorney called two days ago wanting to discuss something. Adam asked if it was urgent. The attorney said it could wait until Monday. That was only one of the appointments on my long list.

I ran my fingers through CJ's hair. His eyelids blinked as the tranquil blue within shone my direction.

"Good morning," I said, landing a kiss on his lips.

CJ reached for my waist and lifted me over him. His grin grew, revealing his dimple, as he leaned forward capturing one nipple and then the other. "I've changed my mind," he said. "I don't want real life. I want to wake every day with your spectacular breasts in my face."

They weren't spectacular. They were small. That's what happened when someone worked out each morning. Lately, my workout had changed forms and partners.

Sitting up on his stomach, I was well aware my bare core was exposed as well as the large erection against my back. Pushing his long hair away from his face, I stared. Next, I ran my fingertips over his shoulders, collarbone, arms, torso, and designs of his tattoos. "I want to remember every defined line—everything about you."

"We have each other's number. I'm open to learning more about Missoula."

I tilted my head to the side. "I'm not really who I've been this week."

"I don't believe you."

"You don't?"

CJ shook his head. "You've shown me the woman you are, Lena. A hunter, a lioness, an absolutely insatiable lover, and a carnivore. You can't convince me that isn't the real Lena."

"Who are you when you're you?"

"This is me. Yes, there's shit in real life, but this is me." He tucked my hair behind my ear. "I'm real. For this week you've reminded me that life does exist beyond work. I'd like to see you again."

Leaning toward the bedside stand, I reached for another condom. Tearing the package with my teeth, I flipped back the covers, revealing the stark beauty of the man in my bed. "I want to see you make love to me."

Taking the condom, CJ covered his erection. Before I realized what happened, he had me on my back, staring up at him. "Hey."

"You like it, Lena. You can't hide that from me. You like to take charge, but you wouldn't want a man who would bend to your every demand."

I swallowed, thinking about what he was saying. "I am a take-charge person. I've had to be."

"I believe you. I bet you're damn good. I know you are. You don't have to be that woman with me. With me, you can enjoy having a man bring you pleasure. You can admit that you like to give up the reins every now and then."

I could admit it. I could confess my desires because at the end of the day, I'd be back in Missoula, and CJ's number would be blocked from my phone. I wasn't happy about either of those decisions, but that was what would happen.

"Tell me what you want," CJ said, his body positioned between my knees, his hardened cock teasing my core.

"Take the reins."

And take them he did.

I couldn't recall a time I'd felt as free as I did, relinquishing control to CJ. He took that power and showed me what it felt like to be thoroughly loved. That wasn't to say I loved him, or he loved me. It meant attended to and cared for. While he wasn't exactly gentle, he in no way abused the power I'd conceded.

On the contrary, he used it wisely and liberally.

When we made the decision to spend our last day somewhere other than the bedroom, I was completely satiated. With his handsome face over mine, CJ smoothed my hair away from my face.

"How was it?"

I stared up into his turquoise orbs. "Awful. I hated every minute."

He nodded with a grin. "I could tell with the vise grip your pussy had on my cock. Oh, and the magical sounds and curses you continually uttered were other hints. I think it was the four orgasms that had me concerned you hated it."

"I think it was five," I said, sensing the warmth in my cheeks. "I lost count."

"The graveyard of condoms on the floor is another good hint that I hated it too."

Reaching up, I laid my palm over his cheek. "You bring out another side of me."

"It's a sensational side. You shouldn't keep it hidden."

"I don't."

Although I protested, I had the epiphany that I did. I'd worked too hard and too long to create the powerhouse that was Lena Montgomery. The woman Logan Butler had thought unworthy of civility was a successful businesswoman who was interviewed by *O Magazine*. During that transformation from victim to aggressor, I built walls.

For the first time, I sensed they were cracking.

CJ kissed me before moving from the bed. "Room service or breakfast by the pool?"

"Pool," I said. "I need to shower first." Rolling to the other side of the bed, I picked up my phone and shook my head. "Oh, it seems if I don't respond to Kelsey's text messages, they are coming in."

CJ looked down at his naked form and over to me with a grin. "Respond. Please respond. Adam hates me."

"He does not."

"Okay, I won't be the one to tell you that he cares about you."

"Of course, he cares. It's his job."

"Okay," CJ said. "It's only his job."

Shaking my head, I moved from the bed and replied, "I don't think of Adam that way. Employees are a hard no with me, a line not to even consider being crossed."

"Just because you don't think of him that way doesn't mean he hasn't."

"I spend too much time with him to even consider what you say could be true."

"Fine, he's only doing his job, and you don't hide this sensational side of yourself from the real world." He tugged my hand. "Finish the text and join me in the shower."

"Whoa, you've had the reins long enough."

CJ flashed his high-voltage smile. "Come take them back."

I shook my head, watching the vision of him walking away toward the shower. The width of his shoulders, the V of his back, and the sensational view of his ass. When the lust settled, I remembered the text.

. . .

"I'm fine. Overslept. We'll be going to breakfast at the infinity pool in thirty minutes." I noticed a still-packaged condom on CJ's side of the bed. Backspacing through thirty, I amended the text. *"In forty-five minutes."*

Eucalyptus-scented steam was beginning to fill the air as I entered the bathroom. Beyond the glass stall, CJ was washing his chest with my bodywash. Opening the glass door, I stepped inside. A laugh escaped my throat as he used his chest to cover me in suds.

"I love the sound of your laugh."

Taking the loofah from him, I began washing myself as I let the warm water rain down on my hair. When I opened my eyes, CJ was holding the condom I'd discreetly placed on the bench within the shower.

"Insatiable," he said in his deep voice.

"I'll even let you keep the reins."

"Forever?" he asked, his eyebrows raised.

"From now until my hair is dried."

"Maybe we should eat at the swim-up bar."

"Don't push me."

Opening the condom, CJ grinned. "That is exactly what you want and what I plan to do." He lowered his lips to the sensitive flesh behind my ear. "Hands on the tile, Lena."

Doing as he said, I peered back at him. "You should know, I told Kelsey we'd be at breakfast in forty-five minutes."

"Sounds like you won't have time to dry your hair."

Chapter Twenty-One

Lena

Present time

CJ.

Everything Jeremy and I had discussed disappeared from my thoughts, obliterated, annihilated. Jeremy and the other man were shaking hands. I heard their voices, but I couldn't pull my eyes away from CJ.

He was even more dashing in a suit. No, nude was the best view.

This wasn't real, a different dimension in time or space. My mind couldn't compute this...this... I wasn't sure what it was.

"Lena." My name rolled smooth as silk off his tongue.

His tongue. My core clenched recalling what he could do with that tongue.

CJ.

Wait.

I shook my head, my shocked stare told everyone who I was speaking to. "You lied about your name?"

"I didn't lie. I go by my initials."

Jeremy and the other man were looking from one of us to the other.

"Do you two know one another?" Jeremy asked.

"We do," CJ replied.

The other man extended his hand toward me. "Ms. Montgomery, I'm Colton Thompson. It's an honor to meet you."

Hearing him speak reminded me of who I was at the moment. I was *the* Lena Montgomery, the owner of Venus and Montgomery Holdings. "Mr. Thompson— Colton," I said as we shook. I turned to CJ. "That must mean that you're Chandler."

His smile quirked the sexy way I knew it did. "And you're Lena Montgomery."

"Tell me you didn't know."

The sunlight coming through the windows reflected in his turquoise stare as he shook his head with a smirk. "I had no idea. And now I'm floored."

Trying to regroup, I turned toward the three

people in the doorway. The look on Kelsey's face was more of entertainment than shock. Adam's expression was as if this was totally predictable. Of course, it was. They knew.

Kelsey had said there was an odd connection.

"We're fine," I said, pulling out a chair across from CJ.

CJ lifted his hand and waved at my security.

Kelsey nodded.

"They knew," I said as I scooted my chair to the table's edge and crossed my ankles beneath the slab of glass.

"They didn't tell me," CJ replied.

"Someone tell me what is happening," Jeremy said, now seated at my side.

Inhaling, I turned to my business partner. "The acquisition is finalized. This has no bearing on that. Regarding what we discussed earlier, I'm going with my first answer."

Jeremy's eyes opened wide. "Why?" When I didn't answer, he turned to the Thompsons. "Could you two excuse us for a moment? Whatever is happening, we need a moment to regroup."

With my jaw rigid and my teeth clenched, I watched as both men on the other side of the table stood. Keeping my stare straight ahead, I observed as

CJ's body elongated into the handsome specimen of man he was. So as not to stare at the part of his body that was now at the table's edge, I looked up, meeting his gaze.

"Lena."

Momentarily closing my eyes with a slight shake of my head, I replied, "Please give us a few minutes."

Staying statuesque, I didn't move until I heard the door latch. When it did, I dropped my forehead to my arm upon the table. At the same second, Jeremy turned on me, his tenor deep, his volume hushed. "What the fuck, Lena? I've never seen you like this. What is happening?"

Moving my head so I could see Jeremy, my voice was soft. "Chandler Thompson is CJ."

It only took Jeremy a second until his eyes opened wide. "Well, isn't that something? You didn't tell me he was young."

"I guess for one week it didn't matter. I don't know his age."

"Thirty-one."

"Shit," I mumbled. "That explains his stamina."

As Jeremy chuckled, I pushed the chair away from the table, stood, and held onto my own hand. Memories were coming at rapid speed as I paced near the window, recollections I'd planned to keep me company on lonely nights. With my head shaking, I tried to articulate my thoughts. "This changes everything." I met Jeremy's gaze. "Under no condition can he—CJ... Chandler—be employed by Venus. I have rules. I have a line. There are people who could say I've conducted business unethically. It might be the truth in some situations." I shook my head. "Involvement with employees has been my hard line. I won't blur that now."

Jeremy crossed his arms over his chest. "You blocked his number, right?"

"Yes."

"You said goodbye and didn't want to see him again."

"Yes, we said goodbye. I didn't block his number because I didn't want to see him, but so I couldn't. Don't you see how this could be construed?"

"That relationship is in the past," Jeremy continued. "This can be a new relationship. A nonsexual one."

I closed my eyes, heat returning to my body at the thought of CJ. Sighing, I opened them and replied honestly. This was Jeremy. He knew me. "I don't know if I can do that." I had an idea. "Maybe now that he knows the connection, he won't want to stay."

"Then we stay with our plan to make him an offer. If he refuses, that's done."

I let my shoulders drop. "What if he doesn't refuse?"

"That's up to you."

Closing my eyes, I let out a long breath. With them opened, I walked back to my chair and sat. "For the record, I hate that you convinced me that we need him."

Jeremy's hand came to my shoulder. "I know you do. You also know my arguments were strong."

"Fine, Architech is now your baby. I'm name only."

Jeremy grinned. "I'm sure that will last too."

Gripping the back of the chair, I said, "Get them back in here, and let's get this done."

By the time we were all four seated, I saw CJ in a new light. Thirty-one years old. The number seemed young, ridiculously young. However, I knew from our one week that number didn't reflect his intellect or genuine protectiveness. From their expressions, I assumed CJ had filled his brother in on our connection.

How much did he share?

This was why I had the damn line.

I addressed the group, "As we're all now aware, CJ —Chandler—and I met recently. And that fact doesn't change that Venus, a subsidiary of Montgomery Holdings, now owns and has complete control over Architech."

CJ's lips quirked.

Was it at my declaration of control?

Ignoring him, I steadied my breathing and gave the speech I had planned before I knew the audience. The deal was done. No need to play hardball. For the next few minutes, I relayed my thoughts and understanding of Architech as well as the vision I had for the future. I shared that besides the art gallery in SoHo, Venus was inundated with inquiries. Finally, I gestured toward Jeremy.

He nodded and pulled the printed list of the employees we were interested in retaining from his satchel and laid it on the table. "We agreed to a thirty-five percent retention. With this list, we are a bit over forty-four percent. As we discussed, our people are currently investigating more economically sound locations. We will commit to retaining the people on this list; however, at the end of the day, it will be their decision to move and of course we will offer a moving stipend."

Jeremy still had his hand over the paper, his fingers splayed.

"You said there are four cities?" Colton asked.

"Yes," I replied, "Missoula, Montana." I did my

best to keep eye contact with Colton, but as I did, I saw the different shade in his orbs. It took all my self-restraint not to turn to the man at his side, the one with the unique color. "Atlanta," I continued, "Indianapolis, and finally, Lansing. As you're aware, due to the earning potential for the people employed by what is currently Architech, the different states are willing to make some tax concessions. We have decided to keep production going here in Austin until we can make the move."

Jeremy pushed the paper across the table.

Both men looked down at it, their eyes scanning from the top to the bottom.

Finally, CJ looked up from the paper. "My name isn't listed."

"You're not an employee," Jeremy said, "not technically. Ms. Montgomery and I spoke at length…"

As Jeremy spoke, CJ's gaze was fixed on the man discussing his future. Another memory returned from CJ's and my one week. I recalled how he seemed sad that he wasn't working with his brother any longer. This is why. His brother didn't die in a tragic fire as a firefighter; no, they sold their business.

To me.

Everyone was looking my direction. I blinked my eyes, hoping I could recall what Jeremy had said.

"I'm sorry."

CJ's expression fell as his face tipped forward.

"Wait," I said, leaning forward. "I'm sorry because I wasn't listening as closely as I should have. What was the question?"

Jeremy's cadence was measured. "Your decision regarding Chandler."

I took a deep breath. "I'll confess it was Jeremy's influence. Chandler, you have convinced Jeremy that you are and will be valuable."

Light returned to his eyes as Colton slapped CJ's shoulder.

Despite the testosterone, I went on, "Your employment, as with everyone else we retain, will be probationary—a period of three months and we reevaluate." I looked to Jeremy and back to CJ. "Our offer is this: you will take on a supervisory role in research and development, one I'd assume that is similar to what you did previously. We plan to hire a CFO and CEO. Our search-and-screen committee has already begun the hunt. You and the CEO will work hand in hand, your focus being on the technology. The CEO's focus will be more production-based, marketing and financial. I will not be involved other than watching the returns. We've already had many customers interested in utilizing your technology." I smiled. "Our technology."

"You won't be involved?" CJ asked.

Shaking my head, I met his gaze. "My focus is on sales and profits. Montgomery Holdings is extremely wide and diverse. I hire the best people to maintain each piece of the puzzle. Jeremy and I work at growing the pieces while making them fit. If that fit isn't right, we move on."

"Nevertheless, if I agree, I'll be working for you."

"Yes," I replied.

"No," Jeremy said at the same time. He went on, "Ultimately, but for the sake of appearance, Architech was purchased by Venus. Venus is only one of the holdings under the Montgomery Holdings umbrella." When no one replied, he continued, "Before I speak to the employees, we'd like your answer, Chandler. Do the two of you have any questions or concerns that we should address?"

CJ's head tilted to the side. "This is what you do?" He was looking at me. "You buy and sell companies as if they mean nothing."

I met his stare, my shoulders squared. "I buy and sell what is promising. Your virtual environment, hard- and software, is truly groundbreaking. It isn't nothing. If it were, we'd dismantle, take the loss, and move on."

CJ's expression softened. "Could that be why

someone is...?" He looked at his brother and back to me. "Why you're in need of Adam and Kelsey?"

"They're investigating that possibility. I've made more enemies than friends."

"Then those people didn't get to know you."

Chapter Twenty-Two

CJ

I couldn't believe Lena was here, yet my senses told me this was real. Not only the sight of her and the sound of her voice, but also the scent of her perfume. Listening to her speak about Architech—our work—was surreal. Her knowledge and expertise were on full display. While I thought the woman I'd met in Cancún was beautiful and enticing, now, I watched as that same person blossomed into more. Despite Lena's savvy, every now and then, her beautiful brown eyes would come my way, showing me a glimpse of the woman who let her guard down.

The business world beyond Architech was a mystery to Colton and me. Once we started getting offers for our technology, we knew we were unprepared for the future. That lack of knowledge was why we chose Venus. Jeremy promised a business model taking Architech beyond our wildest expectations.

Lena was the knowledge behind the model. Once we all sat, I'd quickly typed her full name into an internet search. There was no way to read it all. A few headlines was all it took to show me a glimpse of her success.

Listening and watching, I was in awe of her poise and understanding.

It was more than Lena's confident attitude. Her appearance was different. She was still beautiful, but superficial in a way. Lena didn't need the makeup she was wearing or the power clothes. Maybe to be this person, the one she said she wasn't in Cancún, she did.

"I think we're ready," Jeremy said, standing and extending his hand to Colton and then to me. "Chandler, it would be reassuring to your employees if we could tell them definitively that you will remain."

"It's what I've wanted since the sale was finalized." With my hand still shaking Jeremy's, I stopped and turned to Lena. "I know we're on a time crunch, but could I talk to you...alone?"

"We don't have time," she said matter-of-factly. "We have an over three-hour flight."

"Lena." I said her name with all the emotion I could muster.

The chocolate stare softened, bringing back *my* Lena, the lioness.

She looked at her watch and nodded. "Two minutes."

"Do you want me to wait for you?" Jeremy asked Lena.

"No, go ahead. Kelsey and Adam will stay."

Of course, they will.

As Colton and Jeremy filed from the room and Lena stood, I scanned this new version of the woman I had gotten to know. From her styled hair, white blouse, and all the way to her dark blue skirt and jacket, I saw the powerhouse she was. I knew every inch of what the clothes covered, and yet seeing her like this was a glimpse at the real-life Lena Montgomery. Silence prevailed as I held my tongue, waiting until the door closed and we were alone. Finally, I spoke, "Lena, talk to me."

Lena's head tilted to the side. "CJ, I only have one request."

"You blocked my number."

She straightened her neck and shoulders. "I implore you, don't tell anyone that we...what happened. You have no idea how difficult it is to be taken seriously in this world when you're a woman."

I would never do that, not to Lena, not to any woman.

Taking a step closer, I confessed. "I did a quick search on my phone" —I shrugged— "as inconspicuously as I could. You're a trailblazer."

"No, I'm a" —she smiled— "lioness. I just needed someone to remind me."

"You blocked me," I repeated.

Lena nodded. "I did. Paradise was over. Back to real life."

"Funny thing about real life...I must have done something right because for the second time, the gods have presented me with an amazing woman—the same amazing woman." I wanted to reach out and touch her, to feel the warmth of her soft skin, but I kept my distance. "Lena, I'd like to get a chance to know this side of you."

She shook her head. "Accepting the position with Venus makes you off-limits. My hard line is dating anyone who works for me."

I took a deep breath. "Then I'll tell Jeremy I've decided to decline the offer before he announces it to the masses."

Her soft chocolate eyes opened wide, and her tone filled with empathy. "No. CJ, this company is what you were in your head about that first day. I know that now. You didn't want to sell."

"I didn't want to, but I did. Colton and I agreed to the sale because we believed under Venus what we began could become even more—achieve more than we can comprehend."

She nodded. "It can. It's truly revolutionary. Jeremy was right, having someone who knows the ins and outs is beneficial. Name your salary."

Money?

"I don't need money. Hell, you already paid more than I ever imagined obtaining in a lifetime."

"It's worth that and much, much more."

Staring into her eyes, I said, "I don't want money. I want more than two minutes with you—more than one week. More."

Pink filled Lena's cheeks as she looked down and back up. "I blocked you because saying goodbye once was too difficult. I don't want to say it again."

"Then don't."

Lena shook her head. "I'm too complicated. The stalker thing is only the tip of the iceberg."

"You told me from the beginning that you were trouble. I agreed." I grinned, losing my better judgment and reaching for one of her hands. I hesitated, waiting for her to pull away. When she didn't, I enjoyed her soft touch and went on, "You, Lena Montgomery, are trouble, and the only thing I want is to have the time and opportunity to find out how much trouble." My smile widened. "I've never enjoyed being in trouble as much as I enjoyed being in..." I didn't finish that sentence.

With a quick squeeze, Lena released my hand. "No, CJ. Trust me when I say I'm not worth that sacrifice. You need to accept our offer and stay with the company you love. Jeremy has faith in you."

"Only Jeremy?"

She sighed. "I have faith, CJ. I was attracted to more than your body. You're witty, sincere, intelligent. I had no idea it was you who created the technology behind Architech, but knowing that increases my faith. You're a good man. The future of Architech needs you."

I ran my thumb down her cheek. "Lena, you may be an amazing businesswoman. From what little bit I saw, you are. You, however, have a serious misunderstanding or misjudgment when it comes to your own self-worth. I believe you're worth the sacrifice. I want to find if I'm right on my own. According to your hard line" —I recalled how she said she was better at making rules than following them— "I won't have the chance if I accept the offer to stay."

"Go with your heart, CJ. Your heart is in Architech."

That was a true statement, but couldn't a heart have more than one purpose?

"Are you safe?" I asked, knowing my two minutes had expired. "I've been worried. Not knowing your last name, I had no way to know."

Her eyes darkened. "Safe. At the moment but it's not over."

"I figured," I said, tilting my head toward the door and beyond to her security.

"I've traveled with them for years. It's just more important now."

"It is. I'm glad you have them, but I'd like to know you're safe—a periodic text message or a call."

"I can't. I don't have your number."

"Unblock me. You have it. Even if you deleted it, it's in your phone. You're just afraid to use it."

She stood taller. "I'm not afraid. I'm not prey. I'm practical and methodical down to the most minute detail. It's who I am. I'm not who you think."

Moving closer, I cupped her soft cheek. "You're my lioness." Her eyes closed as she inclined to my touch. "Even a lioness knows fear. It's the instinct that protects her, her cubs, and her pride from other predators."

Inhaling, Lena took a step back. "CJ, it was good to see you again. Let's go into the gathering and set things straight with Architech's employees. You can tell them that you're staying on. From here on out, Jeremy will be your go-to." She lifted her lips to my cheek, letting her lips brush my skin. And then Lena turned and headed toward the door.

Before she turned the knob, I spoke. "I know fear too."

Spinning back, her chocolate gaze met mine.

"Risking everything on Architech was scary." I shook my head. "Colton and I started with very little. The high-end deals that you obviously do on a regular basis scare me." I dropped my hands to my side. "Shit, having the money I made from this sale scares me. I worried it would make people...women...see me differently. I've never had this kind of money, and I don't know what to do with it."

She stood silently, steadfast, as emotions swirled in her light-brown orbs.

"For one week," I went on, "I found a woman who was more than a beautiful distraction. I found a woman I admired for her fortitude, her determination, and her willingness to relinquish control, something that I knew from the moment I saw you was out of your norm."

Lena nodded.

"I'm frightened that if I let that woman slip away, I'll regret it for the rest of my life."

"Look at me." Her voice was strong and hushed. "I'm not a catch, CJ. I'm a workaholic, and a woman hell-bent on success with a side of revenge. I can count my friends on one hand. Over twenty years of therapy bills can support that I'm not a person who opens up easily. Business. That's my life. Failure isn't in my vocabulary. I'm not afraid of it because I've learned through blood, sweat, and tears that not succeeding isn't failing. Giving up is. I won't give up my life to wait at home for a man, doing his dishes or cooking his meals."

"Lord, Lena. You don't know me well, but I'd never assume or ask that. I'm not a misogynist. Yes, I enjoy holding the reins in the bedroom. I also enjoy a woman who knows what she likes and wants. You may have noticed I can share. The women in my life who I care about are equal forces in their relationships. This isn't 1950. I'd never expect you to be a doting woman."

She shook her head. "You would eventually. It's the natural progression. No one can break free." Her gaze narrowed. "Jeremy confided your age to me." She scoffed. "If you'd been born in the suburb of Chicago where I grew up, I could have been your babysitter. Twelve years. That's how much older I am."

Twelve years.

I would never have guessed.

I curled my lips into a grin. "Sounds like some prospective role-playing. My mother says I was stubborn as a child."

Lena let her hands fall to her hips with a sigh. "You're handsome, intuitive, probably a certified genius to create what you've created. You're also protective and a fantastic lover. I'm not a catch, CJ. You are. Meet a nice girl your age and live out your fantasies."

Without another word, Lena turned and reached for the doorknob.

"My fantasies include you."

Lena paused for only a moment before stepping through the threshold. Adam and Kelsey were immediately at her side as she disappeared from my view.

Chapter Twenty-Three

Lena

Flanked on one side by Adam and on the other by Kelsey, we walked in silence. While my mind was doing its best to shut down and reconstruct the walls that had served me so well for many years, I wasn't thinking about the direction we were headed. Instead, I believed that my two most trusted bodyguards wouldn't lead me astray.

As my high-heeled shoes clipped along the hallway floor, my thoughts were back with CJ. Seeing him again was a cataclysmic event—the collision of two worlds with the potential of ruinous results. I needed a minute to regroup before facing a room of eyes all staring at me. Seeing a sign, I sought a moment of reprieve. I stepped away.

"Ma'am," Kelsey said, "Are you all right?"

"Excuse me for a moment."

"I can—"

Kelsey's offer to accompany me disappeared as I stepped into the empty single-person restroom. Illumination filled the small room, triggered by my entry. After securing the bolt lock in the door, I made my way to the vanity, placed my hands on the cool top, and dropped my chin to my chest.

A million questions came in a cyclone, swirling and spinning. More destruction in the wake of the impact.

Why can't our one week be just that?

How is it possible that CJ is the inventor of Architech?

As I steadied my breathing, I lifted my chin, and took in my reflection. "Stop it." My audible advice rang much like the clang of an old schoolhouse bell, ignored by the students playing outside. That was what I wanted, my heart's desire—to ignore the toll of the bell as well as my own advice. I wanted to turn around, go back to CJ, and admit that I wanted more. I would admit to not knowing what more meant. He'd smile and say we could find out together.

That was a fantasy—a dream.

I was never a dreamer.

There was only one person who I knew would stay true to me throughout my life—me. I was too old and set in my ways to betray myself now.

Standing tall, my decision was made.

I wouldn't be the barrier to his dream and possibly lose myself in the process.

CJ wanted to continue with Architech. I would distance myself for his happiness.

After washing my hands, I opened the door and met Adam's and then Kelsey's stare. "I'm good."

"I apologize for not telling—"

Lifting my hand, I stopped Kelsey's apology. "You did as I asked." I turned to Adam. "And you did too. It's time we all move on."

"Ma'am," Adam said with a nod of his head, taking the lead.

"Are you okay?" Kelsey mouthed, no sound coming from her lips.

"I will be." I feigned a grin. "Thank you." I spoke louder to include Adam. "The meeting is probably already underway." I inhaled. "It's a good thing that Jeremy planned on doing the talking."

After taking a staircase down one level, I heard Jeremy's voice. Quietly we approached an open doorway. At the far end of the room was a podium in front of a line of chairs. The group listening had their backs toward us. Seated behind Jeremy were the two Thompsons, an empty chair, and four members of the Montgomery Holdings human resource department. The HR team had been in Austin for over a week, working with the transition.

For only a moment, Jeremy's gaze met mine. Up until this moment, I hadn't truly been listening to what he was saying. I'd been concentrating on avoiding CJ's turquoise orbs.

"...Ms. Lena Montgomery." Jeremy lifted his arm my direction, causing everyone in the room to turn.

Nearly fifty sets of eyes.

I'd spoken to much larger crowds. Those speeches hadn't taken place after a disastrous collision of two worlds. I took a deep breath. "Hello," I said loud enough to be heard. "It's a pleasure to see Architech in action. It is my plan that the ingenuity and brainchild of Colton and C...Chandler Thompson will live on with Venus and prosper under the Montgomery Holdings umbrella." There were murmurs and claps. "Mr. Wilde is your man, the connection to Montgomery. He allowed me to tag along." The room filled with nervous laughter.

"On the contrary," Jeremy said, his deep voice

bellowing through the sound system. "When the boss speaks, I've learned to listen." More laughter, less disingenuous than before.

While I had no plan on taking the chair between CJ and a member of the HR team, I walked toward the front of the room. The room fell silent as I approached the podium. "This is Mr. Wilde's acquisition; however, since I'm here, I want to say that all of us at Montgomery look forward to the future with Architech."

A woman in the front row stood. "Excuse me, Ms. Montgomery. I've been researching your long history. You're impressive."

"Thank you," I acknowledged, knowing from experience that this woman didn't stand with the sole purpose of giving me a compliment.

"Yes, it seems you've made a fortune by acquiring and moving on. That said, I can't help worrying about Architech's future." She spread her arms. "Our future."

I wasn't in the right mindset, yet I knew the ropes. "Please share your concerns." Clasping my hands behind my back, I stood beside Jeremy. He took one step to the side, giving me access to the microphone.

The woman cleared her throat. "How can we be sure that if we make the move, you won't leave us high and dry in a new city?"

"As I'm certain you've learned from our extremely qualified HR team," I began, "Venus is willing to give generous stipends if you are asked to remain with Architech and choose to relocate with the firm. Our investment in Architech is the greatest example I can give you as to our dedication to success. Once each individual is transferred to the new facility, retention will be determined by the work demonstrated." I smiled my best Cheshire-cat grin. "In other words, if expectations are met and exceeded, there is no need to be concerned. If you're already concerned, perhaps taking the severance package is the best option." I turned toward CJ and back to the seated audience. "We're happy to have Chandler Thompson stay on in a familiar capacity to assist with the transition."

The people nodded in agreement.

The warmth behind me alerted me that CJ had stood and was now close, close enough that if I leaned back...

CJ lifted his large hand. "For the record, Venus has presented me with a generous offer. As most of you know, staying on has been my goal. However, in transparency, I will share that I have not accepted it at this time." He looked at me, the turquoise smoldering inside his gaze. "I'm still negotiating."

My lips came together in a straight line as the murmurs grew louder.

Gripping the side of the podium, I addressed the people. "Venus has Architech's future in mind with all hiring decisions. With that, I'll give the microphone back to Mr. Wilde. Thank you."

Going to the back of the room, I stood at Adam's side with my back against the wall, wondering how this happened, how I'd let the lines blur. The business and closed-off part of me, the loudest part of me, was screaming for me to walk away from CJ, to do as I said, offer him the position and watch only from afar.

The newly awakened part of me, the part that remembered what it was like to be in his arms, the expertise of his kiss, and the mastery of his lovemaking, urged me to slow and think. That awakened part was telling me to look at the entire package. Knowing that CJ had created what I was truly astounded by added a new dimension to the man from Cancún.

He wasn't only sexy.

He was smart—beyond smart.

I was lost in my thoughts when everyone began standing and milling about.

"Jeremy will stay with the human resources department for another couple of hours," I said to Adam and

Kelsey. "I'd like to go to the plane and get some work accomplished."

"We'll take you," Adam said, "and one of us will come back for Mr. Wilde."

The three of us were in the front lobby, almost to the front doors, when I heard my name. I knew the voice. The address he used was different.

"Ms. Montgomery?"

Taking a deep breath, I turned. "Mr. Thompson, Mr. Wilde—"

CJ lifted his hand. "I choose you."

The words were like slices through my heart. CJ had no way of knowing my past, the things I'd done to accomplish what I had. He only knew the woman I was for one week. One week out of over twenty years of my climb. A relationship with me would never work.

CJ was a genuinely good man. I knew in my soul that all I would do was tarnish him.

"Mr. Thompson," I said, absent of emotion. "The decision is mine. For the record, I'm choosing you, too. Architech needs you. I made an investment in your technology. Your immense knowledge is invaluable." I lifted my chin toward the staircase. "Those people want you. Please inform Jeremy that you'll stay."

I couldn't be sure if CJ came after me or if Adam's or CJ's better sense stopped him.

All I knew was as I entered the back of the car with Adam and Kelsey in the front, for the first time since Lena Montgomery became a name to be reckoned with, I wished I was someone else.

"Archie and Liz weren't expecting you back so soon. The plane is in the hangar," Adam informed me as we took to the streets of Austin.

"It can stay in the hangar," I said, peering out at the sun-filled sky. "It will be cooler."

"For the air conditioning to run, it can't be in the hangar," Kelsey explained. "I called ahead. Archie is having the plane tugged out onto the tarmac where it can stay until ready to leave."

Exhaling, I acquiesced, "Just get me to the plane."

As the city passed by beyond the windows, I had another thought. It was about my niece. She lived in San Antonio. That was only an hour and fifteen minutes by car. I could get there and be back by the time Jeremy was ready to fly back to Missoula.

I shook my head at the thought.

My niece, Brooklyn, was my sister's daughter and almost thirteen years old. She knew her Aunt Lena cared, but never in thirteen years could I be called a doting aunt. No, Lena Montgomery was too busy for that. To show up unexpectedly...that would probably scare Brooklyn's other aunt. And then there were my sister's in-laws, her ex-husband's parents.

My thoughts were all over the place, not centering on one subject for any length of time when Adam pulled the car into the open gate of the private airport. The Texas heat shimmered above the asphalt, making me want the fresh air of Montana.

I could find solace in my home. I wouldn't let the stalker take that from me.

Adam carried my satchel with my laptop as the three of us walked over the hot pavement toward the Montgomery Holdings business jet. We were almost to the stairs when Liz appeared, her expression odd.

Rushing down the steps, she came our way.

"Liz?" Kelsey questioned.

Her eyes were unusually large. "Mr. Dillon, Archie would like you to come aboard."

My focus went from one person to the next. "What is happening?"

Adam's furrowed brow told me he was as ill-informed as I. "Kelsey," he said, "take Lena back to the car and wait."

"Liz," I questioned, "what is it?"

"Go," Adam said in a more demanding tone.

I stood my ground. "Tell me what is happening, or I'm going up those steps."

Archie appeared, coming around the side of the plane. "I've located the source."

"The source of what?" I asked again.

"Ma'am," Liz said, "After you deboarded and the plane was fueled, Archie and I went into Austin. We didn't know you'd be back this soon. Mr. Wilde had said... it was a long time to wait."

I nodded, not caring what they did with their free time.

"When we received Mr. Dillon's text, we hurried back. There was something...the plane...the smell is... we could only assume it had to do with the heat."

"Smell?" I looked to Adam, Kelsey, and over to Archie as a sickening sensation washed through me. "Is it fish?"

"Yes, ma'am. A whole lot of fish."

"Where?" Adam asked.

"Luggage hold, beneath the fuselage."

"Tropical?" I asked, my volume lowering.

"Ma'am," Liz said, "The smell is horrible. We will need to rent another plane to get you back to Missoula."

"How?" I asked.

Kelsey reached for my arm. "Come with me. Let Adam take care of this. We'll get a plane and get you home."

"Home," I said louder than I should, the term losing its meaning one incident at a time. "Home is where they know I will be. How did they know I was here today, on this flight?"

"Ma'am."

"We only decided this yesterday."

Chapter Twenty-Four

CJ

"You're going to take the offer. Now, you're not going to take it," Colton said, instead of asking.

I stared down at the parking lot from the windows in the conference room, the room where I'd last had Lena to myself. The room where she told me to take the offer—to work for Venus and forget about her.

Practically, it was also a room with furniture, unlike our offices.

"CJ." Colton's volume rose. "Staying with Architech is all you've talked about since Cancún."

I turned to face my brother. "Not *all*."

His lips formed a straight line as he shook his head. "The odds..."

"About as outrageous as two brothers from Ohio hitting it big."

"Buy a lottery ticket, man. You've had lightning strike twice."

Pulling out a chair, I sat at the long glass table. The lingering scent of Lena's perfume came to my senses. The scent she wore today was the same as the first night I went to her suite. Leaning back, I crossed my arms over my chest. The suit coat and tie I'd worn earlier were gone and the cuffs of the shirt were rolled up to my elbows. Extending my legs, I crossed my ankles under the table.

"What are your and Devon's plans?" I asked, suddenly aware I hadn't questioned him earlier.

"We made an offer on that place on Lake Travis."

He'd taken me there before the deal was complete. The home was huge—five bedrooms and five baths, on the water. Well, down a steep cliff and on the water. The original owner was an investor in Architech who no longer needed the extra space. Colton and Devon had been afraid he'd sell before they had cash in hand.

"Andrew didn't sell?"

Colton smiled. "He waited for us. Our offer will make it worth the delay. We're just waiting to hear from the agent. The house has been empty for over six months. Once we have a home base that we want to come back to, we figure we'll travel for a year or so. Then we'll settle down and make a home. You know, little Thompsons running around."

I stared up at my brother, the person I'd looked up to my entire life. "You are thirty-three. Do you think you'll be happy, without goals?"

Colton pulled out the chair across from me and sat. "Devon and I have goals. There are countries and cities all around the world we want to see. We figure if we travel before kids, we can see places we've only read or dreamed about. If we enjoy them, someday, we'll go back with them."

"What's your reason for getting up each morning?"

"Devon."

Taking a deep breath, I contemplated his answer, wondering if it was fair to Devon to take on that responsibility. As much as I wanted a future of some kind with Lena, I knew I wanted more too.

"Do you remember," I asked, "when we both realized that we had something—really something?" My circulation accelerated with each sentence and memory. "Remember how vivid the virtual environment was the first time?"

"I do. It was a once-in-a-lifetime experience."

"I remember being afraid we couldn't recreate it."

"We did. Now it's time to enjoy the fruits of our labor."

Labor?

Colton and I had success, but not the kind that comes from physical labor, not like our father or mother. We invented something valuable.

Were we simply lucky?

Lottery ticket.

"If I could take Lena out of the equation," I said, "which I can't, I don't see myself happy without a tangible goal." I met his gaze. "Lena said she has a hard line when it comes to dating employees." I scoffed. "The good news is that according to her bio, that eliminates possibly thousands of men as competition."

"In other words," Colton said, "if you take the position, Ms. Montgomery is off-limits."

I nodded.

"If you don't take the position, you'll no longer have Architech's continued success and viability as a goal. Will you devote twenty-four seven to pursuing her?"

My nostrils flared as I exhaled. "Yes, but she'd hate me for it."

"Some women would find it flattering."

"Not Lena." I pushed the chair back until it was resting on two legs and looked up at the ceiling.

"You act like you know her, like you're some expert after one week."

My jaw clenched as I let his assumption settle in my thoughts. I lowered my chin to meet his gaze. "You're right. I'm not an expert. I know what I know, and I want to know more." Allowing the chair to drop to four legs, I said, "I'm fucked."

"Don't look at me. I told you to let Architech go. You convinced me you wanted to stay. Now you don't." He shrugged. "I'm out of brotherly advice."

"I mean, I'm fucked because I either take the position and lose any chance with her or don't take it and pursue a fucking successful woman as a jobless man."

Colton smirked. "Yeah, I'm pretty sure she can support you."

What did the bio say about her net worth?

A lot.

"For the first time, one hundred and ten million sounds small."

"It's not," Colton replied. "You're not exactly penniless, or pursuing her for her money. And honestly, since I just met her, I think she's...intimidating."

The hairs on the back of my neck stood to attention. "Why?"

"It's a vibe."

"She's successful and rich, but so is Jeremy and you liked him." I stood. "It's because she's female."

"No. Yes. Listen. I'm not raining on your parade. If you don't feel the ice-queen chill, then I'd say that's a good sign."

I shook my head. "Seriously, fuck you. You heard me talk for two weeks about a woman, a woman I couldn't get out of my head. You meet her and say she's an ice queen." I walked toward the door, ready to end this conversation.

"CJ," Colton called. "I think Lena Montgomery is brilliant. Her understanding of Architech blew me away. That said, yes, she's intimidating. Blame me, not her. It's why I wanted to sell. I knew if we depended on me or you to face someone like her, we'd get taken to the cleaners. Up shit's creek. Choose your metaphor. The lady is good. And seriously, you two meeting without knowledge of one another" —he shrugged— "was a good thing. I'll support you no matter what."

"I've faced her. I held my own."

"Then it's me," Colton replied.

Reaching for my suit coat and tie, I nodded. "I'm headed home."

"Your decision?"

"I told Jeremy I'd give it to him by tomorrow at

noon." I swung the jacket over my shoulder. "A night alone with a bottle of whiskey might help me decide."

"There are better ways, brother."

"Right now, that's the plan." As I opened the door to the hallway, I decided to head toward my old office, maybe for the last time. If I said yes to Venus, the space would be mine again—until the move. As I turned the corner, I stopped short of a head-on collision. Taking a step back, I saw who almost plowed me down. "Adam, what's the rush?"

"I'm looking for Mr. Wilde."

Trying to gauge Adam's emotions was like telling the difference between a partly cloudy day and a mostly sunny day. Nothing. I had nothing. "Is Lena all right?"

"Mr. Wilde?"

My shoulders squared as we met eye to eye. "Where is Lena?"

He lifted his eyebrows. "If Ms. Montgomery wanted you to know her location, she wouldn't have blocked your number."

Asshole.

I gave him the answer to his question, "Jeremy is using Colton's office, this way." I nodded the direction I was headed. "The HR people are in the offices nearby.

They have appointments for at least the next three hours or more."

Adam nodded.

As he turned, I reached for his arm. The stony expression that met mine would have been terrifying if my thoughts weren't on someone more important. "Tell me Lena is safe."

"She's safe. She's headed back to Missoula sooner rather than later. Goodbye, Mr. Thompson."

She's safe.

I let the phrase run on repeat until I caught up to the scene outside my old office in the space separating Colton's from mine. The two men were speaking too low for me to hear the words. That didn't stop me from recognizing the body language. Whatever news Adam was delivering, Jeremy wasn't taking it well.

Ducking into my old office space, I pulled out my phone with a hope and a prayer that if I dialed Lena's number it would connect.

My breath caught at the icon of two missed messages.

How could I miss them?

My phone was on silent for our meetings.

Brushing the icon, I saw they were both from Lena.

Message number one:

"I have your number. You said to message."

I'd said to message about her safety. What the hell happened?

Message number two:

"CJ, if you don't hate me, please call."

I immediately pushed her number.

"CJ." Her voice wasn't of the woman in our building an hour ago; it wasn't even of the woman in Cancún.

"Lena, I just saw your message. What happened?"

The call remained silent until Lena said my name again.

"Whatever you want, I'm here."

"I need to hide. May I hide with you?"

Chapter Twenty-Five

Lena

Seeing CJ's name on the screen, I lowered my volume, put a hand to my other ear, and answered the call. "CJ."

"Lena, I just saw your message."

It was uncanny how the sound of his deep voice steadied me.

"What happened?" he asked

The stalker was getting closer. For the first time since I picked myself up and dusted myself off in an apartment rented by Logan Butler, I was genuinely frightened. Since Kelsey, Adam, and I left the airport, Adam had been insistent on renting a new plane and leaving immediately for Missoula. The Montgomery Holdings business jet was already being attended to by a hired cleaning crew.

A rental plane meant a hired crew. A hired crew consisted of people I didn't know, who may or may not know me.

Could that have been the stalker's plan, have me rent a jet and take me...?

I'd told Adam we needed to find another alternative. Whoever planted the fish in the luggage hold not only knew I was along on this trip with Jeremy but that I was still in Austin. Of course, they would assume my next move was to go home.

Closing my eyes, I felt the walls closing in. The uncertainty was nauseating and the pounding in my temples refused to ease. I forced my thoughts to focus upon the man on the phone. "CJ," I said softer.

"Whatever you want, I'm here."

"I need to hide." To get off the radar. "May I hide with you?"

The time between my question and his answer could have been too short to record, and yet it seemed like an eternity, the culmination of years of self-reliance slipping away, my success whittled down to life and death. With few friends to turn to and my rejection of CJ earlier in the day, this was probably not the right move. He deserved the right to tell me no.

"Yes," he said, conviction growing in his voice. "Where are you? I can come get you."

"I'm here, at Architech."

"I just saw Adam with Jeremy."

"Yes, we're waiting for Adam in the car."

"What happened?"

I looked at Kelsey, still in the front seat. Involving CJ was my idea and mine alone. Kelsey didn't approve, reminding me about my stance on employees. I was certain Adam would approve even less. That didn't matter. I was the boss, and at the moment, I would do things my way. "I'll fill you in. I'm with Kelsey in the parking lot. If you give me your address, they can take me there."

"Shit, Lena. I'm here. I'll take you."

It went against every rule and every measure of safety, and yet I wanted to go with him. "Kelsey will bring me inside. Where can I meet you?"

"Have her bring you around to the back of the building. The parking lot is smaller back there. My car is the Range Rover. You can't miss it."

I covered the phone and spoke to Kelsey. "Take me around back."

She shook her head. "Ma'am, Adam will be here in a minute. He's in charge."

Straightening my neck, I replied, "No, I'm in charge. Take me around the back of this building now."

Getting out of the passenger side Kelsey walked around the car to the driver's seat.

I spoke into the phone. "We're on our way."

"I'm already headed down," CJ said.

"Thank you." I disconnected the call.

As Kelsey began to drive, her gaze met mine in the rearview mirror. "We need to check out his house."

"No," I said, my resolve returning. "No one except you, Jeremy, Adam, and Colton Thompson know CJ's and my history. No one. Other than the acquisition, there's no connection to the two of us. The stalker expects me to either stay in Austin at a hotel, rent a plane, or fly commercial. If the stalker knows I'm here, he or she is watching us. Drop me off with CJ, and you and Adam get rooms, three of them, in Austin. Jeremy can do whatever he wants. A day. Two days. I don't know. Let's see if the stalker makes a move."

Kelsey's lips pursed. "Ma'am, you are our job." Her tone softened. "We do care."

"I know that, Kelsey. I care for the two of you."

"You're asking us to wait for a move while leaving you unprotected?"

"This has to end," I said, sensing my own desperation. "You need to work with Adam and the rest of your team to find out how information is getting out. I hate to think someone on my team is guilty, but it is the only explanation."

My earlier rebuttal of CJ evaporated from my thoughts as he came into view. Tall and solid, his wide shoulders were no longer covered by a suit coat, and the sleeves of his shirt were rolled to his elbows, displaying his toned forearms that exhibited only a snippet of his natural beauty and tattooed artwork. With his dark hair hanging near his chin, concern showed in his expression.

Kelsey stopped the car. Before she could get out, CJ was at my side, opening the door. If his turquoise orbs were the Caribbean Sea, the waters were rough and the skies stormy.

He offered me his hand. "You'll be safe with me."

Placing my palm in his, the strength I needed flowed from him to me. "I believe you. That's why I asked." Standing on the hot concrete, I felt stifling air surround us. Looking up, I pledged, "I promise this will not affect your position."

"I don't give a fuck about a job right now." CJ stood tall and looked in all directions. "Come on. Are you being watched?"

"I don't know."

"Lena...Ms. Montgomery."

We turned to Kelsey. "I'll call you."

"CJ," she said. "I need your address."

As he started to speak, I interrupted. "Go to the hotel. Three rooms. Make a show of renting another plane. Be visible."

"CJ, your address," she repeated.

He wrapped his arm around me and ushered me to the passenger side door. As he helped me inside, he asked in a whisper, "Do you not want her to know?"

"I don't know what to think anymore."

With a nod, he closed the door. I watched for a moment as the two spoke to one another. He stood a head taller than Kelsey and somehow, I knew I trusted them both. CJ returned to the vehicle as Kelsey got in the rental and drove away, I'd assume back to the place we were meant to meet Adam.

Once CJ was back inside the car, he hit the locks and reached over, covering my hand with his. "I gave her my address."

I nodded.

His grin quirked. "They'd be terrible security if they couldn't figure it out."

"I guess that's true. I'm sorry to involve you in this."

CJ put the vehicle in gear. "Your timing is perfect. Full disclosure, I'm Chandler Johns Thompson." He flashed his smile before we pulled out onto a busy street. "My friends call me CJ. I just sold my company.

So as luck would have it, my schedule is free to be involved."

With a sigh, I laid my head back against the seat. "Talk to me."

A lump filled my throat with the realization that CJ was willing to risk everything for me. I turned toward him as my vision blurred, and my emotions bubbled within me. "I was awful to you. I didn't..."

CJ returned his hand to my thigh. "You weren't terrible. I believe you used the word practical. You didn't scare me away."

"I'm glad. I think."

"Talk to me," he said again.

For the next fifteen minutes, as CJ navigated the streets of Austin, I recounted the last few days. Fighting back tears that I haven't shed in years, I told him about the man in New York and about today's discovery. While he drove, I'd had my attention on my story. Now, as I looked around, trees were more plentiful than buildings.

"How far do you live from Architech?" I asked.

"Less than ten minutes on a bad day."

I turned toward him. "Wait, where are we going?"

His cheeks rose as he flashed his handsome smile. "I gave Kelsey my address. She or Adam could have found it in a matter of minutes or faster. I have a two-bedroom apartment, nothing spectacular. I've been too in my head about Architech and this woman I met in Cancún to actively spend my new fortune."

"We aren't going to your place. Where are we going?"

"My brother has been more engaged with the prospect of having expendable income. He and my sister-in-law made an offer on a house on Lake Travis, west of the city. It's in a gated community and has some land. As I was running to find you, Colton told me their offer was accepted."

My forehead furrowed. "We're going to their house?"

"It isn't theirs yet. Don't you see? If we were watched and anyone knows you're with me, they'll never find us. The house isn't in Colton and Devon's name yet. Only the realtors know it's sold. We'll be safe."

"On a lake and secluded," I said, thinking of one of my few friends. "I have a friend with a home on Lake Superior. It's beautiful up there."

"Lake Travis isn't a Great Lake, but in my opinion, it's beautiful." CJ turned my direction as the highways turned to streets. "Trust me, Lena."

"I do."

Chapter Twenty-Six

CJ

Wrapped around her slender wrist, Lena's watch caught my attention. Slowing the Range Rover, I pulled to the side of the road, the gravel crunching under the weight of the tires.

"What?" she asked, her eyes wide. "Why did you stop?"

"Your watch." I lifted my left arm. "If it's the same as mine, you can be tracked."

"Yes, but only by my security."

"Lena, if you truly want to hide, we can't be wearing these watches. We can turn off the tracking on our phones, but the watches are a completely different animal, even with the factory-installed *Find Me* feature turned off, with the right knowledge you can still be tracked."

Indecision showed in her beautiful features, the worry lines near her eyes and the way her lips were pressed together.

I lifted Lena's chin, bringing her gaze to mine. The chocolate orbs swirled with emotions. I'd told her earlier that she'd been afraid to have my number. That wasn't true fear; it was her way of shielding herself. What churned before me was visible dread, a chilled-to-the-bone terror. "You reached out to me. You wouldn't have done that if you didn't trust me."

"I trust you. I trust my security."

"Who has access to that watch?"

"The entire team."

"Adam and Kelsey?"

She shook her head. "No, many more. Adam and Kelsey travel with me the most, but there's a team."

"Who knew you were coming to Austin? Colton and I didn't hear that Jeremy wasn't alone until your plane landed."

"Jeremy. I told him yesterday that I wanted to come. Adam was with me at the time. He knew. Jeremy said he'd call Kelsey. By the time we took off this morning, everyone on the team..." Her words faded as she fumbled with the band with shaking fingers.

"Let me," I said, placing her wrist on my knee and

unfastening the clasp. Once it was off, I did the same with mine, taking it off. "Where is your phone?"

Lena reached for her purse and opened a flap, revealing her phone.

"Turn off the tracking."

She punched a four-digit code into her phone and went to settings. Pulling my phone from my pocket, I checked the tracking capability. It was off, the way I have always kept it.

"Done," she said.

"May I see?"

"I know how to work my phone."

"I'm sure you do. Are you confident someone hasn't added another tracking app?"

Lena sighed and handed me her phone.

Swiping the screen, I entered her four-digit code.

"How do you know that?"

"You just did it."

"And you remember?" she asked.

"I'm kind of weird about numbers." I smiled. "Yes, I remembered."

It took a minute to scan all her apps, but in the end, I found two additional programs that could pinpoint her phone's location with significant accuracy. "Two was smart," I said, giving her back her phone. "Most people would quit after finding one."

"I'm sure it's extra precaution."

"Turning off the apps is our extra precaution."

Looking around, I realized we were closer to Colton's new home than I wanted anyone to know. The thing about Lake Travis was that it was a reservoir for the Colorado River with over two hundred and fifty miles of shoreline.

"We're going to go on a bit of a wild goose chase, or maybe we're the geese."

"CJ, I want to trust my team."

"This isn't saying they're not trustworthy. It's to protect you."

Lena nodded.

By the time we were miles beyond Colton's home, I drove into Dink Pearson Park, parking along the well-packed dirt road. "Come with me?" I said, looking over at Lena.

She was stepping down from the Range Rover, her shapely legs visible below her skirt as I came around the vehicle. Without assistance, she landed her high heels on the dirt. Taking off her blazer, she tossed it back in the vehicle and stood in her skirt and white blouse.

Offering her my hand, Lena took it as we walked toward the shoreline of a small inlet.

Lena lifted her face to the summer evening breeze

as she looked around. "It's hot and flat."

"You're very observant."

"No, I'm tired," she said with a chuckle. "Missoula has mountains, snowcapped even in the summer. This heat is stifling, almost worse than Chicago."

"Missoula is sounding more and more appealing."

"We might be moving Architech there."

Reaching into my shirt pocket, I handed Lena her watch. "I hope you're not attached."

"To a watch." She shook her head.

As I unclasped my own watchband, I started to toss it into the water and stopped. "Damn thing is waterproof."

"Mine too."

Dropping mine to the ground, I used the heel of my shoe and smashed the face before picking it up and tossing it in the water. When I looked over, Lena handed me hers.

"You're better at the smashing thing."

"Are you one hundred percent certain you're okay with me doing this?"

"Yes."

The face cracked and went black before I handed it back. With one look my direction, she reeled back her arm and threw it into the water. As her watch sank below the surface, small ripples blended into the water's texture.

Lena exhaled. "It's freeing."

Wrapping my arm around her, I pulled Lena to me until she lifted her chin. "You'll be free, free of this lunatic, free of being watched."

"No. It's my life."

"It doesn't have to be."

She lowered her forehead to my chest and surrounded my torso with her arms. Just the two of us in Dink Pearson Park, Lena Montgomery's persona faded, and the woman inside took the first step of freedom. When she looked up, her brown gaze glistened with moisture. "Thank you."

"Thank you for trusting me."

"It's crazy, I know. We don't really know one another."

My grin grew. "We don't, but I know I want to learn more, all the magical sides of Lena Montgomery."

She lowered her forehead to my chest. Her words came out muffled. "I don't know who to trust anymore."

"Come on," I said, keeping my arm around her and leading her to my vehicle.

Taking both paved and dirt roads, I drove in circles, in the hope that we weren't being followed. As the sky darkened, I pulled into a small store, told Lena to wait, and went inside. When I returned, I had four bags of groceries and a twelve-pack of water.

When her gaze met mine, I grinned. "This is my first hideout, but I don't think letting you starve would be a good start."

Her smile faded as she lifted her phone screen my direction. "It's blowing up with calls and texts from Adam, Kelsey, Jeremy, and now others on the security team."

"Have you responded?"

She shook her head.

"Respond. Tell them you're safe. If you don't, Adam will have me on the top-ten wanted list before we get a chance to eat the packaged deli meat."

As I started the car, Lena hit a number on her screen. After a moment, she spoke, "I'm safe, Jeremy."

Interesting that she'd call him before Adam or Kelsey.

Her gaze came my way. "I do. I really do. Trust me on this." There were pauses as Jeremy spoke. When Lena disconnected the call, she lowered the phone to her lap and sighed.

"I'm curious," I said. "Why you called him and not Kelsey or Adam?"

"Jeremy started out working for me, years and

years ago, before either Adam or Kelsey. Our relationship has changed, morphed into something beyond work."

"Lovers?" I asked, unsure that it was any of my business but unable to stop the question.

Lena shrugged. "Nothing serious. We are better as cohorts."

"He called you his boss at Architech today."

"I'd say that Jeremy Wilde is more of an independent contractor. He gets me."

The sky beyond the windshield had begun to darken. "I think I get you."

Lena reached over and placed her hand on my thigh. "I think you do too."

Fuck.

Seeing her slender fingers outstretched over my pant leg and feeling her touch, I was more determined than ever that Lena Montgomery would stay safe under my watch. I also had hope that she'd just given me the answer to her hard line.

Pulling up to a large gate with stone pillars on each side, I entered a code. The gate before us began to move.

"How?" she asked.

"Colton brought me here to show me the house a few weeks ago."

Lena's lips curled upward. "And you remember the code."

I nodded. "Numbers, remember."

"How are we getting in the house?"

"The realtor lockbox also works with a code."

"I'm glad you're good with numbers. I meant what I said earlier, CJ, your technology—what you and Colton created— is a world changer."

Colton's new home sat on over six acres of property, tucked high above the water's edge. The five-bedroom home was mostly windows. As we approached, the security lights illuminated the grounds while the inside remained dark.

As I pulled onto the concrete and stone driveway separating the house and the garages, Lena gripped my forearm. "Are you sure it's safe?"

I wanted to be certain.

"Yes, but I'd rather be absolutely sure." Leaning over, I hit the button on my glove compartment. The small door opened, revealing a Glock 19 pistol.

"You have a gun?" she asked.

"It's registered and yes." I'd never shot more than targets, but I was more than competent at the shooting range.

Lena's gaze met mine. "I'm glad."

"Stay behind me."

"I don't want you to get hurt."

"Give me the reins, Lena. I promise I'll give them back."

The fear in her expression eased as she nodded.

Chapter Twenty-Seven

Lena

My racing circulation had me on the verge of fainting as my pulse thumped in my ears, drowning out all rational thought. Step by step, I walked behind CJ toward the large house. Stone slabs created a walking path leading to the main entry. With each step, another light came on, illuminating the outside and keeping the inside behind the unblocked windows a mystery.

"What if someone is inside?" I asked, keeping my volume low.

"No one should be. It's been empty for months."

"Should be? That isn't reassuring." When CJ turned back toward me, I asked, "Is there a security system?"

"Yes. Set to a code."

"What if they changed it?"

"Then we go to plan B."

I scoffed. "You always have a plan B."

"I haven't thought this one out yet, but yeah, I like to leave my options open."

Once we were on the front porch, I turned the flashlight app from my phone on and shone the beam toward the realtor lockbox. I held my breath until the hinge released, and CJ opened the box, revealing a key.

"So far, so good," he said with a grin.

The natural noises set my nerves on high alert. Around us the trees rustled in the breeze. Above, owls hooted, and bats flapped their wings. A low hum filled the air as CJ opened the door inward. Quickly, he went to a keypad near the door and entered another code.

The hum ceased.

"It worked," he said. Then speaking louder, he called out, "Hello."

CJ's greeting echoed in the empty entry, bouncing off the hardwood floor and ceiling and ricocheting off the glass walls. After removing the lockbox from the outside door handle and locking the door from within, CJ reached for my hand. With our steps in sync, we went to the right, into a large master bedroom suite.

Walls were either wood, stone, or glass. Everything was very open with natural materials. Furniture was present in a staged way that realtors do. There was nothing personal. The room and large attached bath were sleek, modern, and sterile.

After turning on lights and checking every nook and cranny, we walked back through the entryway toward the main house. I stopped for a moment. "The outside lights have gone out."

"Motion detectors, I'd assume."

That made sense.

As the sky darkened, and the inside brightness grew, the windows became mirrors. Through the next archway, CJ led us to the left. We discovered two more bedrooms, each with attached bathrooms. He searched in every closet, behind every shower door, and under every bed. Back out to the main hallway we turned left. The ceiling heightened as we entered a large open kitchen. Edison lightbulbs strung fourteen to fifteen feet above glistened off the quartz counters. The rectangular island contained a deep sink and was covered with a butcher-block top. The far quartz counter seconded as a breakfast bar with five high-backed stools separating the kitchen from the family room.

The main hall was all glass. CJ said it faced the lake. I'd have to believe him as nothing could be seen through the panes except darkness.

We kept walking, turning on light after light until we came to the far end of the house, a wide-open living room with a slate-stone fireplace, one that I imagined would be nice if the outside temperature wasn't still near ninety.

Setting the safety, CJ placed the pistol on a table and reached for my hands. "We're alone, Lena. You're safe here."

"Does Colton know we're at his new home?"

"Not yet. I have about fifty voice messages from him. I say first, I bring in the things I purchased at the store, we eat something, and settle in. Then I'll give him a call." His turquoise stare shimmered in all the artificial lighting. "You asked me for my help. Now, I want to discuss our next move. You're more in tune with your threat level. Tell me what you know, and let's figure this out together."

"How do you remember all those numbers?" I asked. It was hardly the most important information at the second. Nonetheless, I was curious and impressed. "How many times have you been here?"

"I don't know how I recall numbers. I just do.

Colton can do it too. And" —CJ grinned— "this is my second visit."

"Are you a genius?" When his smile quirked, I justified my question. "Are you? I'm serious. The technology. The codes. You saw your brother enter them once. You saw me unlock my phone once. You're very analytical."

"And hungry. How about you?"

"Yes, first..." Wrapping my arms around CJ's torso, I held tight, listening to the steady yet rapid beat of his heart, feeling the rise and fall of his chest, and sensing his determination. His arms followed suit, encircling me. With his chin on the top of my head, he reassured me again that we were alone and safe.

Lifting my chin, I met his gaze. "I feel the need to apologize. I'm not a woman who expects anyone, a man or woman, to pick up the pieces of her life and put them back together."

"I'm not picking up pieces nor am I putting them back together." CJ teased a rogue strand of hair away from my face with his finger. "I'm just holding the glue, Lena. Don't apologize for asking for or accepting help. You said it today."

I was listening.

CJ went on, "You said you buy companies, not to run them yourself or micromanage. You employ competent people who will strengthen your invest-ment." He shrugged. "Maybe not a direct quote, I was a little preoccupied with memories as I listened."

"I was preoccupied with memories as I spoke. You could say I got up and talked about the benefits of pet adoptions or green energy. At this point, I'd have to agree with you." I shook my head. "I don't remember."

"I remember your confidence, your knowledge." He reached for my chin and held it in his grasp. "You trust others with your investments. Trust me with your greatest asset." When I didn't respond, he tilted his forehead down to mine. "You, Lena. Trust me with you."

A few minutes later, I stood in the open doorway, watching as CJ pulled his Range Rover into one of the garages. With the garage door closing behind him, he walked toward me, the bags of groceries hanging from one hand and the twelve pack of water under his other arm.

Once he was inside, I asked, "Do they ever stock the bar for showings?"

"I don't know. We can look." After setting every-thing on the kitchen island, CJ walked toward the far end of the house. "There isn't anyone close, but if we don't want every boat on the lake to know we're here, we should turn off some of the lights."

As he went about the house, I pulled the groceries from the bags. No one would call me a good cook. In reality, I never tried. Madison, my sister, was more of a homemaker. That didn't mean that I'd starve if left to my own devices. Based on the ingredients CJ bought, it appeared that turkey on wheat bread was our dinner. He even had an assortment of condiment packages. I grinned when I discovered the yogurt containers. He had breakfast covered and remembered what I'd eaten in Cancún.

With no plates, I opened the paper towels and laid a piece of bread on each. Searching the kitchen drawers, I found a stash of individual plastic silverware place settings. Our dinner was almost prepared when CJ appeared, coming from the way of the master suite.

"You didn't need to make me a sandwich."

I pushed the paper towel toward him. "I'm not a chef. But I can manage a sandwich." Suddenly, what I'd said earlier in the day came back. "I'm not someone who takes care of others, but I can be a team player. You are hiding me away. I can make us something to eat."

Sitting side by side at the breakfast bar, we ate our dinner and drank from water bottles.

With all that had happened, I found myself surprisingly calm.

"I checked in the master bath," he said. "There are towels if you want to take a shower."

Looking down at my blouse and skirt, I said, "This is all I have. No other clothes."

CJ chuckled. "Who knew hiding out was so complicated? There should be a checklist of supplies."

"I wasn't planning on staying the night. This was a one-day trip." Marveling at the house around us, I asked, "How many children do Colton and his wife have?"

"None. Why?"

"The house. It's large."

CJ got down from his stool and collected the remains of our meal. "The man who had this house built was an early investor in Architech. He and his wife have kids and grandkids. A year ago, his wife passed away. I would imagine this house was too full of memories. I don't know what Colton offered, but I know he and Devon—that's my sister-in-law—were excited to purchase it. They plan to travel and then come back and settle down."

Smiling, I hummed as I sat back. "I have one sibling. A sister. She was always the one with the dream of a family. She never cared about money or a career. I didn't agree with her goals, but I respected her choices." I shrugged. "They weren't mine."

"What's your sister's name?"

"Madison."

"Did she get what she wanted?"

I shook my head. "It didn't exactly work out."

"Do you want to tell me what happened?"

"Not really," I answered honestly. "She has a daughter. My niece lives in San Antonio. Her other aunt, Brooklyn's father's sister, is raising her." I looked out at the wall of windows where CJ said the lake would be visible in the morning. "I let my sister down."

CJ came back, taking the chair to my side as he turned his attention on me. "How?"

"I moved on. I felt shut out, and I didn't try to fight. Instead, I worked night and day to turn everything into more. More money. More power. More influence. I'd been beaten down, and I refused to stay that way." My tone saddened. "In the process, I missed that my sister was ill and needed me."

"Did she ask for your help?"

I shook my head again.

CJ's warm hand covered mine, which was suddenly cold. "It doesn't sound like you let her down. If she didn't tell you..."

"I didn't try to see. I should have." I took in a deep breath. "I'm helping her now."

"That's what matters."

"She's in prison, CJ." I couldn't say what made me blurt out the information, but I did. "She is lost in her own mind. I wasn't the only one who let her down, but I deserve a portion of the blame. Now, I'm doing all I can to get her the help she needs."

CJ sat back, exhaling. "What about your niece?"

"I've offered her other aunt financial support. She has sole custody."

His gaze narrowed. "Your brother-in-law?"

"Ex-brother-in-law. He's in prison."

"Did he hurt your sister?"

"Yes, but that's not why he's in prison." I turned my hand until our palms met and our fingers intertwined. "I told you. I'm a whole lot of trouble."

"I don't believe in guilt by association. I also don't believe that by concentrating on yourself and your career that you are culpable for your sister's choices."

"How are you so young and so wise?" I asked.

"My mom has told me I have an old soul. I'm not sure what that means. As to wisdom, I'll give credit to years of watching *Law and Order*. I used to think I wanted to be a prosecuting attorney."

"What happened?"

His cheeks rose. "I preferred video games to studying. Then I realized I wanted more out of the games."

"That's how Architech was born."

CJ nodded. "I guess law school isn't out of the question now."

"Stay with Venus."

He lifted our joined hands, bringing mine to his lips. "I won't let you go again, Lena."

Chapter Twenty-Eight

CJ

I wanted nothing more than to wrap Lena in my arms and hold her all night long, helping her to forget about the asshole with the grudge, the one threatening her life.

"We need to discuss the threat level."

"DEFCON 2, maybe 1."

Letting out a sigh, I asked, "Is there a pattern?"

Lena shook her head. "That's what makes it the most unnerving."

"Yet nothing happened in Cancún."

She grinned. "Something happened but not with my stalker. The threats even stopped in Missoula while I was away."

"The threat isn't only in Missoula. The man...in New York."

"Right. There was one time in..." She paused. "I travel so much that cities get mixed up. I think it was in Atlanta. Room service delivered my meal." She looked down and took a deep breath, her breasts pressing against her silk top. "When I lifted the dome there was a clown fish on top of my meal."

"What the fuck? How?"

Lena shrugged. "The delivery man said he'd never left the cart unattended. The kitchen staff claimed innocence. But there it was, taunting me, telling me I was being watched."

I forced a smile. "The only one watching you right now is me, and let me tell you, you're a stunning sight."

"Yeah," she said with a scoff, "I'm sure. I think I might like that shower you mentioned."

It was then I remembered something. "I have a softball bag in my Range Rover."

Lena grinned. "I think our chances are better with the gun than a bat, or are you suggesting a game? I was an all-star catcher in my day."

"Now that's not listed on your bio."

"It was in high school, you know, when you were in diapers."

I stood taller. "I'll have you know, I was potty-trained at a younger-than-average age. My mom says it's because I was trying to keep up with Colton."

"I stand corrected," she said with a grin.

"In that bag, I have extra shirts and shorts for when I don't have time to go home to change. As our luck continues to hold out, they are clean." I scrunched my nose. "I definitely wouldn't offer if they weren't."

Her gaze fluttered over me. "I could wear a t-shirt to bed."

"Yeah, I was thinking in preparation for bed. For the actual bedtime" —I lowered my timbre— "I'd like to recommend an alternative dress code."

She looked down at her phone. "I should check in with Adam or Kelsey."

That wasn't the response I was going for, but she was probably right.

"I need to call Colton." I met her soft stare. "Are you going to disclose our location?"

Lena shook her head. "I'll tell them what I told Jeremy—I'm safe."

"Okay." I stepped down from the stool and leaned in, leaving a kiss on Lena's cheek. "I'll go get that bag and be right back."

"Hurry back."

There weren't words to describe what I saw in her expression. The person who was doing this to Lena needed to be caught and deserved to be imprisoned. I didn't know what transpired with her sister and brother-in-law, but I knew whoever this was sending Lena the messages was the cause of the anguish in her eyes. I also knew I'd do whatever I could to take that torment away.

The air beyond the air-conditioned house was heavy and hot despite the setting of the sun. After entering the garage, I lifted the hatch on the Range Rover and removed my softball bag. It was about three feet long with a place for my bat and a rather cavernous interior, filled with more than a few shirts. While I played on one team, I was a regular sub for a few others. It could be said that I had a competitive streak in me.

Closing the hatch and the garage, I went along the stone path toward the front door. There, standing at the window with one arm around her midsection, was Lena. She had her other hand near her chin. She'd taken off the high heels as soon as we arrived at the house. In bare feet and her blouse and skirt, I didn't see the ice queen Colton saw. No, I saw a strong, successful woman who wanted the comfort that came with handing over the reins.

Once back inside, I locked the door and again brushed a kiss over her hair. "I thought of something else I have in here."

I tilted my head toward the master bedroom suite.

Together we walked down the hall until we were within the suite. Placing the bag on the bed, I unzipped the top. Digging to the right, I found a roll of toilet paper and presented it to Lena. "For emergency use. Some ballparks are...well, they need help."

Laughter filled the room. "I hadn't thought about it, but I'm glad you have it."

Next, I pulled out a travel bag with hotel-sized soaps, shampoos, conditioners, and lotions. There was also a full-sized deodorant and toothbrush and tooth-paste. "I collect most of this when I travel and throw it in here."

It was her turn to scrunch her nose. "Share a toothbrush?"

I turned and pulled her flush against me. "I've had my lips on your pussy and you've deep-throated my cock. I think sharing a toothbrush is acceptable."

As I spoke, a rosy hue filled her cheeks. Her eyelashes veiled her gaze for only a moment until she replied, "When you put it like that..."

"Let's see what else is in here." I removed three t-shirts all in different colors and a pair of nylon shorts. There were also cleats and long socks.

"It's like Mary Poppins's bag."

I narrowed my gaze. "English nanny?"

"How can you be a genius and not know who Mary Poppins is?"

"I know who she is. I've never watched the movie."

Lena's smile grew as she shook her head. "Just when I was beginning to believe you were this well-rounded man."

"Give me your thoughts on Mewtwo, Dragonite, or Tangela." When Lena's expression blanked, I added, "Pikachu?"

Pressing her lips together, Lena shook her head. "I admit to having never heard those words before in my entire life."

"They're Pokémon."

"What are Pokémon?"

A laugh bubbled from my throat. "You teach me about Mary Poppins. I'll teach you about Pokémon."

"Do I want to know what that is?"

"Not tonight, but if we ever go out with Colton and Devon, it would be best to at least pretend to understand what they're saying."

"Your brother and sister-in-law?"

"Yes."

She took a step back. "CJ, let's take this a day at a time. Once my life isn't being threatened daily, I may consider a merger of real life and" —she motioned between us— "whatever this is."

"A merger," I said with a grin.

"Maybe."

"Listen, I still haven't dug fully into your bio, but if Lena Montgomery is mentioning a merger, I think I should hire a representative to investigate the fine print."

"Absolutely not." Her smile grew and her head tilted to the side. "I will only negotiate the merger with one person and one person only." She took a step toward me and placed her palm over my chest. "And you should be warned, I have a reputation."

Cupping her cheeks, I brought her lips to mine. Turning my face and hers, we melded together. The bedroom filled with her moans as our tongues fought for the lead. When the kiss ended, Lena's lips were pinkened and puffy and curved into the perfect smile.

"You should be warned," I said, lowering my tenor. "I know the woman behind the name. She's my lioness, and I'm not afraid to use that knowledge to my advantage."

Lena grinned. "You fight dirty. I like that."

This was the Lena I wanted to keep, the one who pushed back with equal force and desire, the one who could let down her walls and live in the moment. Colton was wrong. There was no ice in the veins of the woman before me. On the contrary, there was fire.

Lena took one of my shirts and the travel kit. "I'm going to take you up on that shower."

"Do you want company?"

"After the shower." She looked at the screen of her phone. "Shit. First, I should contact Adam. The poor man will have a meltdown if I don't."

"I'll give you some privacy." I walked toward the bedroom door. "I need to call Colton. You've at least been in contact with Jeremy, Kelsey, and Adam. I haven't talked to anyone."

She nodded as she took a seat on the side of the bed.

One last glance told me that the lioness who had made a brief appearance was gone, replaced by a combination of the strong, successful woman and the terrorized prey of some lunatic. Closing the bedroom door, I walked to the kitchen.

With all the interior lights out, I could now see beyond the windowpanes. These windows looked out onto the driveway and the wooded area around the house. The trees in the distance were lit by a blue hue from the large moon hanging low on the horizon.

Colton answered on the second ring. "What the fuck have you done?"

I waited, trying to decipher his question.

"CJ. Do you have any idea of the trouble you've caused?"

"How did I cause trouble?"

Colton's voice was hushed. "Ms. Montgomery's security is livid. They've accused you of stalking and tormenting her. Tell me that's not true."

"They accused *me*?"

"Mr. Dillon said Ms. Montgomery would not want the publicity, but if you don't produce her by nine tomorrow morning, he'll be forced to involve the police."

"He's an asshole and has never liked me."

Colton replied, "This isn't a popularity contest. Where is she—Ms. Montgomery?"

"She's safe. I don't know what you know, but someone has been stalking her—long before we met— and no, it's not me. Whoever it is continues to leave her calling cards. I'm not going into detail, but something happened today. She texted me."

"She blocked your number."

"And she unblocked it," I said. "She asked for my help, and I said yes."

"Lena Montgomery who has a full-time security team contacted *you* because why? You're some kind of superhero and I didn't know. Why would anyone believe that?" Before I could respond, my brother went on, "Listen, CJ. That's not the story I'm hearing."

"It's not a story. I was with her when she called Jeremy. He knows she's safe. She later called Kelsey or Adam; those are the two that follow her everywhere."

"From what I've heard, Jeremy went back to Missoula. The other two are still here and pretending Ms. Montgomery is too, to the public. In private, saying that man isn't happy doesn't begin to cover it."

Of course, he wasn't happy. Adam has had something against me from day one. "Kelsey brought Lena to me."

"Tell me where you are, where you took her," Colton said.

I hesitated.

"What the fuck? You won't tell me?"

"Someone is fucking with her, Colton. There's someone close to her that can't be trusted. The less you know, the safer you are."

"Then tell me, why would you write that tweet? If this goes public..."

"What tweet? The deal is done. You have your money. I have mine." I stood to my feet; the phone plastered to my ear. "Shit, this isn't about the money. I don't give a damn if somehow the deal is retracted. I only care that Lena is safe."

"That isn't your job..."

His voice trailed away as I met the gaze of the woman standing silently near the counter. There was something in the way she stood there in the darkness.

"Colt, I need to go. Tell anyone you want that I called. Ms. Montgomery is safe. That's all anyone needs to know."

I hit the disconnect button before he could respond.

Turning off my phone, I tossed it on the counter and went to Lena. "What happened?"

Chapter Twenty-Nine

Lena

"Did you mean what you just said?" I asked.

In the dark kitchen, CJ was pressed against me, his arms on either side, pinning me next to the counter. It was impossible not to react to the heat from his touch or the hardness of his body as his hips pressed against mine. I wanted to reach up, frame his scruffy cheeks, and pull his lips to mine. The only thing stopping me was the voice in my head.

"What did I say?" His questioning response was deep and measured, his words vibrating through his body to mine.

"About the money. That you don't care."

"Lena, I don't give a fuck about money. This is the first time I've ever had it, but it doesn't change who I am. My brother is afraid..." He took a little step back, relieving the growing pressure building within me. "... He said Adam thinks I kidnapped you, took you against your will."

"I just read the same thing."

"From?"

"Adam. It's ridiculous. Kelsey was there."

"Did he tell you that?" I asked.

"I haven't called; instead, I started reading his text messages. He's saying they found out more information about you." I took a deep breath and stared up at CJ. "Adam thinks you went to Cancún to meet me."

"He's a fucking liar. You know why I was there. I was upset about selling Architech."

"And what better revenge than to seduce and expose the person responsible for the sale."

CJ took a step back and ran his fingers through his hair. In the moonlight shining through the windows, I saw his clenched jaw and his bulged bicep as he turned a complete circle. When CJ stopped, his volume was raised. "*I* was responsible for the sale. Colton and me. We agreed to sell. I had seller's remorse, but revenge... that's not who I am. What the fuck was I supposed to expose?"

I reached for my phone from the counter and brought it to life. The screenshot I showed was from his twitter feed. CJ took the phone from my hands and stared at the screen.

When he looked up, his expression was one of shock. "Lena, that's my Twitter account, but fuck, I rarely post. I didn't post that. Hell, no one follows me."

"They do now. If not you, who?"

The tweet tagged me, saying CJ knew the secret to my success, knew it firsthand, and he should have held out for more negotiation. The pic was of us together in the cabana in Cancún. It was too far away to see what was happening, but it didn't take a wild imagination to figure it out.

"Fuck if I know," he said in exasperation. "I'm in the cabana. I obviously didn't take the picture."

"Who did you pay?" I asked. "One of the waitresses or waiters? How much did you pay them?"

"Stop, Lena." CJ gripped my shoulders. "I. Didn't. Do. That."

"I can't stay here."

"Did you tell Adam where we are?"

"No. I don't know where we are. I texted saying I'd talk to you and get him the location. It was clear in his messages that he's upset about the watch. He asked why I took it off and asked if it was your idea."

"And you told him it was me."

I shook my head. "I haven't responded, but it made me think. It was you. It was your idea."

CJ inhaled as he paced back and forth like a caged animal. "Someone close to you is involved. According to you, that watch was connected to an untold number of security employees. Yes, it was my idea."

I looked down at my feet, unsure what or who to believe.

"Lena," CJ said, "Adam's jealous."

I snapped my face up. "What?"

"He's jealous of me. He has been since you invited me to your suite in Cancún."

"That's ridiculous. You're not the first man I've been with since Adam's worked for me."

"That's none of my business," CJ said. His face tilted. "Do you see the way he looks at you?"

"No. There's nothing like that between us."

"Between you. That doesn't mean it isn't one-sided."

I walked over to the breakfast bar and sat, lowering my forehead to the counter. When I looked up, CJ was across from me. Even in the moonlight I felt his stare, his presence. Just like this afternoon near the podium, I knew he was there before he spoke. It was like hearing his voice on the phone earlier today; it steadied me.

Had I let my body overrule my better judgment?

"Talk to me, Lena. Don't overthink. Go with your gut. It's gotten you to where you are now."

"Adam doesn't think you're the stalker. He thinks you took advantage of the knowledge I shared and tried to scare me."

"How? I didn't know you were in Austin until after the plane landed."

"The fish were believed to have been put in the cargo hold while I was at Architech. You could have hired someone."

"So the fuck could he."

I sat taller. "Adam wouldn't do that."

"The list of possibilities is limitless." CJ reached across the counter and covered my hand with his. "I wouldn't do that, with the fish. You know in your heart. You wouldn't have texted me to help you if you didn't trust me. Lena, I would rather die than scare you."

With his hand holding mine, CJ came around the counter and tugged me from the chair. In one fell swoop, he lifted me from the ground, cradling me against his chest. "You're as light as a feather."

"Hardly." I squirmed. "Put me down."

"No."

I blinked my eyes at his refusal. "Excuse me."

"I didn't take you against your will. You know that."

"The watch…"

"It was for your safety."

"Did you tell Colton that we're at his new house?"

CJ shook his head. "No. You and I, we're taking the rest of the night off from real life. You texted Adam, and you spoke to Kelsey earlier."

I nodded.

"I didn't tweet, Lena. I'll delete it right now."

Leaning my head against his chest, I sighed. "I hate publicity. Even good publicity turns bad. This started bad, meaning it will only get worse. You can delete it, but screenshots last forever."

CJ sat me on the counter and reached for his phone. I watched as the phone came to life, and he swiped the screens. Finally, he handed me the phone. "I don't even have Twitter on my phone. Look."

I took the phone from his hand and read through each app and edge widget. No Twitter. No Facebook. "But it is your account?"

"Yes. I made it years ago. When was the tweet posted?"

Tilting my head toward the other side of the kitchen, I answered, "I don't know. Let me look at the screenshot again."

CJ brought my phone to me. I pulled up the text message. "It says five hours ago."

"I was with you five hours ago with no other access to the internet than my phone."

I tried to reason. "It was five hours ago when Adam got the screenshot. I don't know when that was. It could have been yesterday or weeks ago while we were in Cancún."

"And no one thought to notify you sooner?"

A new thought came to me. "What if the stalker was there? What if he saw us?"

CJ took the phone from my grasp, hit the button on the side. "We'll turn both phones off and save battery. Lena, you need a break from all of this. Hell, after only part of a day, I need a break." He grinned, offering me his hand. "Come with me. Trust me. And let me take your mind off real life."

"You should run."

His eyes opened wide. "From you?"

I nodded. "Like I said, I'm trouble."

"What is the saying...something about women making history?"

"Well-behaved women seldom make history. It's a quote from Professor Laurel Thatcher Ulrich, written in an article about Puritan funeral services. It's been misinterpreted. She meant that well-behaved women should make history, not to encourage women to be rebels or less well-behaved."

CJ grinned. "I like the misinterpretation."

"I'm rarely well-behaved."

"Good." Again, he extended his hand. "Show me what you've got."

"You've seen it." I placed my hand in his and jumped down from the counter.

He tugged my hand toward the bedroom. "Show me again."

Chapter Thirty

CJ

I woke wrapped around Lena's sensual body. Using my body as a shield or a cover wasn't completely my doing. The positioning happened as we surrendered to sleep, a surrender neither of us was willing to do until we were both too exhausted to continue. The tycoon businesswoman whose name sent shock waves through the financial community, burrowed next to me until her petite form was cocooned by mine.

Lifting my head on my elbow, I stared down at Lena, marveling at the soundness of her slumber. I didn't know Lena well enough to know if this was her normal. I knew this was how she slept in Cancún. Granted, our sleepy nights were most always preluded by a vigorous workout—workouts.

Last night, as I tugged Lena's hand toward the bedroom, I had one objective—to keep her mind on the present. Judging by her current state of unconsciousness, I succeeded at least in some form. As we both peeled the clothes off the other, I relinquished the reins.

Our disrobing came in bursts of energy punctuated by kisses and caresses. One minute we were soaring at two hundred miles an hour around a fast oval track. The next, we were strolling hand in hand along the shore in Cancún.

Lena's pale flesh glowed in the moonlight as she stood completely naked before me. There was an obvious push and pull happening within her. The woman who stayed in control needed that power, desired evidence that she was still the woman others saw her to be. At the same time, the more transparent woman, the one who allowed me to see behind the walls of her own doing, desired to be released.

It was a tightrope of sorts.

When I reached for her shoulders, Lena stiffened, her body a rod. As I let go, she came to life, shining a teasing smile as she gently pushed me back on the bed and made her way onto my lap.

I'd never been with a woman like Lena, a woman

who craved control while at the same time yearned for submission.

It wasn't hot.

It was a fucking forest fire, an inferno.

Give and take.

With her chocolate eyes swirling with emotion, she kept her stare locked on mine as she sheathed me with her core, little by little. Our breathing labored as she worked to accommodate me in her tight pussy. With each inch her breasts pushed forward and pulled back. She snagged her bottom lip between her teeth as whimpers and moans filled the room. All the while Lena was the choreographer, the lead in the dance.

The vision was spectacular beyond my imagination.

I had a front-row seat to a master.

Forget the front row, I was there as her fingernails grasped my shoulders and her core gripped my cock. I was close enough to feel her warm breath as she writhed against my shoulders, her arms around my neck, her intimate noises a melody for my ears only.

After what I believed was her second or third orgasm, Lena's soft body collapsed in my arms with our connection unsevered.

"Tell me what you want," I said, my warm breath on her neck, hoping that she wasn't ready for sleep.

Taking what remained of her strength, Lena lifted

her face and met my gaze. Her smile shone. "I want you to take the reins."

"Are you sure?"

"I'm sure."

From the ringmaster to the lioness, Lena morphed.

Yes, she still had her power, but in the hands of the ringmaster, she was able to acquiesce. Now, with the knowledge of who Lena was, her momentary submission was all the more erotic, a gift I would never abuse.

Ask any trainer who has worked with lions and lionesses. The first rule was to not show fear. If the predator sensed indecision, the exercise was over, and the ringmaster became food. No part of me feared the sensational woman in my hands.

Adore.

Protect.

Pleasure.

The list went on and on until our satiated bodies were spent, our minds a mush of endorphins, and our limbs a tangled mess. It was then that my lioness burrowed next to me beneath the blankets we'd compiled and settled in for the night.

Currently, the sky beyond the large windows was lightening with pink clouds along the horizon. Teasing Lena's deep-red hair away from her face, I stared at the whole of her as if she were a masterpiece I wanted to memorize. Every valley and peak were a vision to behold.

The thought wasn't conscious, the way my circulation rerouted. It was primitive, the attraction between a man and woman—a transformation that has occurred since the dawn of time. Simply having her near caused my cock to swell.

Lena's eyelids fluttered as my touch roamed over her arms, waist, and hips. Not fully awake, she rolled, giving me access to her core. Kissing my way down her toned stomach, I settled between her legs. Her body convulsed at my first lick. It wasn't an orgasm, more a response to my welcomed invasion.

My name echoed off the windows and wood paneling as I held tight to the reins from the night before. Pleas as well as curses rang forth as I held her bucking hips in place, and her grip of the blankets intensified. It was as she stiffened that I climbed up, finding my place, and sliding into her wet core.

Buried to the root, I peppered her lips and nose with kisses. "Good morning."

Lena's light-brown gaze glistened. Her cheeks rose and her lips curled as she focused on me. "Good morning." She looked around the room as best as she could while pinned down. "What time is it?"

I laid a finger to her lips. "Shh. It's not time to leave our bubble."

"CJ." Real life was infiltrating her thoughts; I saw it in the turbulence of her stare.

"I'm not letting you up until you come two more times."

"Two?"

I scoffed as I had her full attention. "Me, Lena. That's all you should be thinking about."

"I've already...I can't promise two."

Lowering my lips to her neck, I continued my rain of kisses on her sensitive skin as my hips rhythmically eased my cock in and out. Leaning down further, I sucked one nipple and the next. Lena's protests, or more accurately, insecurities, melted away as we both found our mountain.

When I lifted my torso and our gazes met, Lena's smile was ear to ear.

"Sorry, CJ. I don't think you have it in you for one more."

Holding tight to her hips, I spun until I was the one pinned to the mattress, and Lena was over me. "You do."

Her hands were on my shoulders, her round breasts in my face as she laughed. "I'm supposed to work for my own orgasm?"

"I'm giving you back the reins. Unless you don't think you can do it."

The soft brown gaze over me sparkled as Lena eased herself up and back down until she found the rhythm, the one that arched her back and tightened her grip. This was another astounding display of sensuality. It took all my self-control not to submit to the pleasure before she did.

As we both shuddered, I wrapped my arms around her, pulling her down until our bodies molded together, transfixed by the heat of the encounter.

Holding her against me, I marveled, "You're so fucking gorgeous when you come."

"I wasn't sure, but then..."

Her words continued, but it wasn't what she said. It was that reality that Lena was sharing, even something as personal as her insecurity about her ability to orgasm. In a way I couldn't describe, her confession felt monumental while rather trivial at the same time.

I smoothed her hair away from her face. "You did it, Lena. There is nothing you can't do."

The shimmer in her expression waned.

"I wish I could keep you away from real life all the time."

Lena nodded, still in my arms. "I wish that too."

Her palm ran over my scratchy jaw. "I made the right decision messaging you."

"I'll always be there for you."

"I wish that could work."

Twisting until Lena was lying against the pillow with a deep-red halo of hair, I kissed her nose. "It can. I figured it out."

"What have you figured out?"

Chapter Thirty-One

Lena

"I have an idea," CJ said. "It's based on something you said."

Deciding to bask in the postcoital glow for another minute as warmth filled my cheeks, I asked, "Was it before or after you handed back the reins?"

CJ's grin grew. "You know, the lines are blurry."

Lifting my face, I brushed his lips with mine. "They can't be. Not having a sexual encounter or relationship with an employee is my line. It's been a hard line for as long as I can remember. If I don't obey my own rules, no one else will."

His turquoise stare focused on me. "Lena, whatever this is between us is special. I've never felt this way."

No, because you're a baby.

I didn't say that.

"Give it twelve more years."

He sat taller. "I'm hardly a virgin."

"That's not what I meant."

His gaze drilled into me. "Have you? Felt this way? You have the twelve years. Tell me, am I just another man in a long succession...?"

I sat up against the headboard. "No and yes. There have been many men. I won't lie to you." Inhaling, I looked down at my hands and back up, fearful to admit that CJ was special, but also unwilling to lie to him. "You're right. There's something about you that's different—special. I haven't investigated my feelings enough to know what that is." Squaring my shoulders, I pulled a blanket over my breasts. "Listen to me. You're a good man. I trust you. I feel like I can be open around you. With you, I'm free to think and do what I may not otherwise do, but that doesn't trump the fact that I'm not a good person. I've put my success over everything and everyone. CJ..." No. "Chandler, you shouldn't be tied down with a woman like me. Look for someone your own age, someone without a history of destruction. Please stay with Architech."

Sitting up, he untangled himself from the blankets and stood. In two strides he was at the large windows. Beyond the panes, the sky was filling with a light blue.

Turning my way, CJ gave me a full-frontal view of his sculptured, Adonis-like body complete with the erect appendage.

Before I could give that more thought, he spoke.

"Didn't you say that you and Jeremy have a history...an intimate history?"

I shrugged. "Yes, but it's only been a physical thing. Our friendship isn't about sex."

"What did you say his role has shifted into at Montgomery Holdings?"

Trying to recall my words, I finally said, "An independent contractor. That isn't the way it always plays out legally...taxes and all."

CJ's face lightened, his smile brightening. "I don't want to be employed by Venus. I want to be a subcontractor. I'll work for myself, just as I've done. I'll offer my services to Venus in an overseeing role with Architech."

I shook my head. "Jeremy and I don't come home to one another every night."

CJ was back by the bed, sitting at my side. "Are you saying that's what you'd like, to come home to one another?"

"Yes. No." I lifted my hands to my face and sighed. "It would never work. I'm an awful person. When I'm mad, I'm explosive. When I'm stressed, I overwork and under sleep. I've been known to eat too little and drink too much. I'm up every morning before dawn working out, and I appreciate my alone time."

"I'm all for working out in the morning," he smiled. "Today's workout was especially enjoyable. We buy a house big enough for us to have our own space."

As much as I was intrigued by what CJ was proposing, there was another pressing matter. That of my stalker. That of my life.

My gaze met CJ's. "If he wins... If whoever is stalking me succeeds, I want you to know that you are my silver lining in all this mess. You have made my final weeks and hours unforgettable."

CJ stood. "Don't talk that way. You're not allowed to discuss your final weeks and hours until you're ninety-five and I'm eighty-three. Women live longer, you know?"

Getting out of the bed, I placed my hands on CJ's strong arm, lifted myself to my tiptoes, and brushed his cheek with a kiss. "I mean it. Thank you."

"Lena."

"I'm going to shower."

"Coffee?"

I nodded. "I saw you had yogurt. Once I'm showered and dressed, it is time to face real life."

"You're not facing it alone."

"I am. It's how I've always been."

CJ reached for my hand. "Not now. I'm not negotiating. You're more important than Architech. Until this person is found, you're stuck with me. I didn't send that tweet, but you know what? Since it's out there, fuck them. I, Chandler Johns Thompson, am in an undefined relationship with you, Lena Montgomery."

"Lena Anne," I said, unable to stop sharing.

He tugged me closer, pulling me against his chest. I needed to crane my neck upward to see his turquoise stare. "Lena Anne, this is me taking the reins, if only for a moment."

The conviction in his voice, in every word, resonated through me, through my circulation, into every cell.

"I don't care how badass you are or need to be. Sometimes it's nice to be able to let your guard down. You can do that with me. Today. Tomorrow. Forever. I'll never think less of you or believe you're less because you enjoy the freedom of submission."

I laughed. "CJ, I'm not submissive."

"Neither am I. But I can share and so far, you've shown me a willingness to do the same."

"I-I..." The realization hit that what CJ was saying had more than a grain of truth. I took a deep breath as I stepped away. "Shower. Coffee. Then real life."

Making my way into the attached bathroom, I met my reflection.

My fingers skirted over the pinkened splotches on my skin. My mind filled with the cause—CJ's scratchy jaw and cheeks, and the way his attentions abraded my flesh while at the same time bringing me pleasure.

CJ was special.

I could admit that to myself in my own head.

I'd admitted it to him because if the stalker wasn't stopped, I didn't want to die without CJ knowing the truth. Holding back tears that I rarely shed, I went to the glass stall and turned on the shower.

With my face under the hot spray, I gave in.

Into the realization that I may have met the man I could share the rest of my life with.

Into the reality that it could be too late.

Into the grasp that my quest for success was at the root of my stalker's motivation.

Into the understanding that accepting CJ's offer—or demand—would put him in danger.

Into the decision that I needed to sever whatever this was that we had.

Into the anguish that I didn't want it to end.

Those and other thoughts overwhelmed me as I succumbed to the mass of all I'd done. Funny, I'd carried the weight forever without feeling the burden, and now, as the walls around my heart crumbled, the load felt too heavy to bear.

I was lost in my thoughts not hearing the bathroom door open or noticing that I was no longer alone. With tears in my eyes, misery in my heart, and terror in my thoughts, as the large hand reached for my shoulder, I screamed. My self-defense training came back as the butt of my palm shot toward his nose.

Chapter Thirty-Two

CJ

"Whoa," I said, ducking and narrowly avoiding a broken nose. Quick reactions and years of bad softball pitches had taught me well.

"CJ." Lena's eyes opened wide as she began to tremble. "I'm sorry."

Wrapping her in my arms, Lena collapsed against me, her body shuddering with sobs. For more time than I knew, I held her, my lioness. There were many things I didn't know about Lena Montgomery, things I was willing to learn. However, what I did know, in the depth of my soul, was that the woman in Cancún was the real Lena. The woman in the boardroom was the real Lena. This woman, the one whose anguish cut at my heart, wasn't. Or at least she wasn't the woman Lena often allowed to be seen.

As her breathing evened, I reached for a small bottle of shampoo. Squirting a dollop into the palm of my hand, I took a step back and massaged it into her hair.

"CJ."

"Shh," I whispered. "Let me pamper you."

Turning, she looked up at me with a shattered expression. "I don't deserve that."

My cheeks lifted with my grin. "It's not your decision, Ms. Montgomery. It's mine."

I'd never washed or tended to another person, and yet as Lena acquiesced, something within me took over. From the shampoo and conditioner to the bodywash, I cared for her, gently caressing and molding, giving her not only my attention, but offering her my strength.

Once I'd towel dried her hair and had her wrapped in another towel, Lena looked up at me. Her tears had ceased, leaving her eyes red and puffy. "I feel like I say it a lot, but CJ, this isn't me."

"You're multidimensional. I'm absolutely fascinated with each and every one of them."

With a towel around my waist, I led us to the kitchen where I had a pot of coffee brewing. It was a good thing coffee was a constant at open houses as it was the only thing of substance that we had in abundance.

Sitting at the breakfast bar, I placed a warm mug in front of Lena along with a container of yogurt and a plastic spoon. For the longest time, she sat unmoving.

"I can feed you," I offered.

It was as if my words brought her out of her thoughts.

"I sold myself."

"What?"

Lena squared her shoulders. "When I was twenty years old, my parents died in an automobile accident."

"Lena, I'm..."

She lifted her hand. "Please, CJ, let me tell you who I really am. I want you to understand why you need to leave."

"I'm not leaving."

She nodded. "You will."

I swiveled my stool to give Lena my full attention.

"Have you ever heard of a company called Infidelity?"

"A company? No."

She smirked. "It no longer exists. Back in its day, it was an escort service, of sorts. Contracts were for a year. They claimed to not sell sex but rather companionship." She sighed. "They sold sex."

"You worked for this company?" I asked, trying to wrap my head around what she was saying.

"When my parents died, the two of us were left alone. Since my sister is two years younger, I was supposed to take care of her. No one expects to die at their age, yet our parents were wise. They left us with a substantial life insurance policy and some inheritance. I was young, but I knew what was needed to provide for Madison and me. I met an attorney." She inhaled. "His name is Logan Butler."

Lena paused.

I shook my head. "I've never heard of him."

She nodded. "He was in Chicago—is in Chicago. He was supposed to be my knight in shining armor. He promised me the stars, moon, and sky. He was going to invest our money, making Madison and I set for life."

My stomach twisted. "He didn't."

"No," Lena said, "he didn't. He also began a relationship with me. I trusted him." She sat taller. "By the time I realized what he'd done, our money was gone. Madison wanted to study art. I was desperate. I went to Infidelity. They promised housing and what I believed at the time to be a lot of money. My only stipulation was that I wouldn't be paired with Logan."

"And what happened?"

"My contract was purchased by a man named Avery Nicholson."

"I don't know him," I said.

Lena shrugged. "Hell, I barely did. He signed the contract, showed proof of an apartment in Chicago where I could live, and paid for the year."

I fucking hated hearing this story. At the same time, I knew Lena needed to share. If she thought this was going to make me run, she was wrong. "What happened?"

"Nicholson handed me over to Logan Butler. I don't even know their whole agreement. By purchasing my contract, Avery repaid a debt he had with Butler or something. I never saw him again." Lena shook her head and lifted her mug of coffee for the first time. "It wasn't enough for Butler to steal our future; he was determined to ruin me."

A grin came to my lips. "He failed, Lena. You're not ruined."

"It happened more than once, but one night was particularly bad." She took a drink of the coffee and left the rim of the mug near her lips. "He beat me."

As she spoke, red like I'd never known infiltrated my thoughts. I didn't know this man, but I'd happily return the favor.

"I wanted to kill him." She turned my direction. "I had a gun. I was ready."

"I believe you. You're also not in prison. Or is that part of the story?"

"No. A friend, one of the few I have, came to my aid. He got me out of the apartment. Compared to the Butlers, at the time, my friend and I were nothing." She grinned. "Infidelity no longer exists because my friend and I refused to be nothing." She shrugged. "We're both doing okay."

Okay?

"Would I know your friend's name?"

"Maybe. If I live, maybe you two could meet."

"I'd like that."

"CJ, I picked myself up that night. I had my friend's help, but I made the decision that nothing would stop me. I'd been dabbling in investing. You see, Logan Butler underestimated me. He made mistakes, leaving accounts open on his laptop, assuming I was too stupid or ignorant to understand. I watched and learned. Life became my teacher. That night I walked away with months remaining on my contract and a few million dollars in overseas accounts."

A smile tugged at my lips. "You stole from him?"

"I did."

"Did he ever find out?"

"I think he knew, but we had the goods on him for other indefensible acts. I made it my life's goal to succeed, to make a name of Lena Montgomery. Recently, I was part of a conspiracy to bring attention to Logan's brother and sister-in-law."

"Attention?"

"The SEC received a reliable tip. A grand jury has filed an indictment. There's no guarantee that they'll be found guilty, but they should. It's the publicity that has hurt. Deals that were in progress with Marlin and Gwen Butler have been rescinded. The publicity is affecting Logan too. Until my stalker, I was popping popcorn and watching their world shatter."

I stood, securing my towel. "It's got to be them, the people responsible for the fish and candy."

Lena shook her head. "Logan was our first thought. If he's doing this, he's doing it from afar. Logan would also know that Madison isn't in Missoula. He wouldn't make that mistake. He's only the first of people who probably deserves to hate me." Picking up the plastic spoon, Lena turned to me. "Run, CJ. This is who I am. I'm a thief and a prostitute."

"Listen to me," I said. "It sounds to me like you're a fighter, a survivor, and a winner. You're a lioness who has had to kill to survive."

"Murder is one crime I'm not guilty of."

I reached for Lena's cheeks and tipped my forehead to hers. "If that story was supposed to scare me away, I'm sorry. You didn't succeed. I choose to see a strong, successful woman who has had to overcome extreme obstacles." I kissed her lips. "I've been a little busy to follow up on my research about Lena Montgomery, but I'd guess what you just told me isn't in your biography."

She shook her head. "Infidelity was…" She inhaled. "They had clients from all walks of life from celebrities and politicians, to royalty and entrepreneurs, to sports icons. The average person would be gobsmacked by the revelation they'd been deceived or people they admired paid for such services. Those records are sealed tight. If the company did anything right, it was to go down without publicity."

"So, what you're saying is that you trust me."

"No, yes. You're only one of a handful of people who know that story."

My smile grew. "Thank you for trusting me."

Lena sighed. "I think I told you because I'm saying you don't want this." Lena gestured to herself. "I'm not exactly the woman you want to bring home to your mom."

A scoff escaped my lips. "My mom is actually pretty cool herself. I'd never share anything you didn't want shared, but I'd bet my mom would admire your fortitude. My dad too."

"CJ, I can't and won't darken you."

"Since I saw you in that big white hat, sexy bikini, and large sunglasses, you, Lena, have been a light that beckons me. I had no idea that you became who you are without the backing of family or family money. Hell, I admire you even more. Colton and I come from average parents—cool parents—but average. Having the money from the sale of Architech made me feel like a fish out of water." I scrunched my nose. "Sorry. Bad metaphor."

Lena smiled.

"I love your smile. I also like the fact that I know you aren't interested in me because of that money." I laughed. "I got it from you."

"I learned the hard way that involving myself with a man for his money is the wrong reason."

"What do you look for in a man?" I asked.

"I don't."

"Humor me."

Lena stepped down from the stool. "Everything I see in you. I wasn't looking, but now that you're here, you're too good to be true. You're everything I never knew I wanted."

"Get dressed," I said. "I'm not scared away. I'd

gladly keep you here naked forever, but we're not letting this person win. And you're not getting rid of me."

"People will think that the sale of Architech…"

I placed my finger on her lips. "Do you, Lena Montgomery, truly give a shit what people think?"

"Some people."

"Who?"

"I care what people think of you and your brother."

Tugging at the top of her towel, I grinned. "If I go down in history as the man who snagged the strong, resilient, successful" —I let her towel fall— "sexy, and insatiable Lena Montgomery, I'm all right with it."

Chapter Thirty-Three

Lena

I watched out the windows of CJ's Range Rover as he drove us to his apartment. I'd called Adam, alerting both he and Kelsey that we'd be arriving by ten in the morning. We'd yet to disclose our hiding place. Maybe it was because there was part of me who wanted to return, to eat turkey sandwiches and yogurt, to avoid real life and embrace the silver lining.

My phone vibrated. I looked down at the message and turned to CJ. "They're in your apartment."

"That's a little disheartening. So much for locks."

"Since Adam told us he was going to do it, I hope you're not thinking of pressing charges for breaking and entering."

CJ reached over and splayed his fingers on my thigh. I was wearing the same skirt and blouse from yesterday. While I'd never gotten the chance to wear CJ's t-shirts, he was. His suit from yesterday was replaced with nylon shorts and an orange t-shirt with the name of a restaurant on the front.

"No charges," he said with a grin. "I'd rather they're certain the apartment is secure."

"What if they're being watched?"

CJ's grip of my skirt-covered thigh tightened. "Yesterday, Colton asked me why anyone would believe that you contacted me when you have an entire security team. He asked if I had superpowers he didn't know about."

Laying my hand over his, I mused, "You do."

"I do?"

"The superpower of making me feel safe and allowing me to forget about the mountain of troubles in my life, even if only for a night. I slept better last night than I have since returning from Cancún."

"I'd like to combine my superpowers with Adam, Kelsey, and others in your security." He grinned. "For the record, I'm not working in a paid capacity, so no need to worry about your hard line."

Sighing, I let my gaze drift back onto the streets of Austin. "I've been thinking about your proposal."

"And..." he encouraged.

"If I make it out of this...I'm game for the idea of you working with Venus, not for Venus."

"You will—make it out."

"If I don't," I went on, "please stay with Architech. Jeremy can take Architech to the masses, but he'll need you there at his side."

"You told me about this Butler guy. Do any other adversaries come to mind?"

I shook my head. "I've been racking my brain. No one else comes to mind except my ex-brother-in-law. "

"Madison's ex-husband? Didn't you say he's in prison?"

"He is. I would assume that gives him connections, but to be honest, he doesn't have the means to pay. The man in New York had been promised five thousand dollars."

"You said you helped to dissolve the company Infidelity. Could someone from there be seeking revenge?"

"It was long ago. Water under the bridge." I turned to CJ. "I appreciate your trying to help."

"No, this isn't done. My years of experience watching *Law and Order* are kicking in. I say we sit down and go through the last few years of business history."

"My team..."

"Fresh eyes."

My temples pounded as I considered his offer.

"We're here," CJ said, pulling into a large apartment complex. "It's nothing exciting. The house on Lake Travis is much nicer."

I sent a text to Adam, saying we were close and then looked at the buildings, all similar in appearance. "What floor do you live on?"

"Second floor."

As CJ parked the Range Rover in an empty space, the door to the building ahead of us opened, and Adam came out. He was at my door before CJ could turn off the vehicle. That meant that the door was still locked when Adam tried the handle. I turned back to CJ.

"We'll keep you safe," he said.

"I-I hate being dependent."

"You're not, Lena. You're the boss, the person in control. That doesn't mean you don't need them. They care about you and need you too. It goes both ways."

Inhaling, I nodded. "You don't need me. I'm the worst thing for you."

"You're right. I don't need you. I want you." He reached for my hand. "The want is strong enough to become a need. For *you*." He emphasized the word. "Your laugh, your smile, your everything."

"I'm sorry I got you involved in this."

"I'm not."

With a nod, I reached for the door handle, unlocking the door. Instantly, Adam had me at his side, ushering me into the building. I turned back in time to see someone stop CJ near his vehicle.

"Wait," I said.

"This way," Adam said, taking me down a hallway and through another door.

As Adam opened the door, I realized we weren't going to CJ's apartment but out to a waiting SUV. My feet stopped as I reached out to the doorjamb. "What the hell are you doing?"

"Our jobs," Adam said. "I don't trust Mr. Thompson."

"I do."

Adam's light-blue eyes narrowed. "Ms. Montgomery, get in the car, and let us tell you what we've learned."

My thoughts went back to the man I saw with CJ. "Who is with CJ?"

"Mathew. We called in a few more members of the team."

Why didn't I recognize him?

"Is he...? What is Mathew doing with CJ?"

The driver's side of the black SUV opened, and Kelsey appeared. "Please, Lena. Listen to us."

"Where are you taking me?"

"We have somewhere safe," Kelsey said.

"Is CJ okay?" I asked with one more look over my shoulder.

Adam replied as we started moving toward the SUV. "If he's innocent, he will be."

Before entering the back seat where Adam was holding the door, I said, "He is innocent."

"Please," he said, nodding toward the interior.

Once we were all inside the SUV and Kelsey began driving, I sent CJ a text message.

"I'm not sure what is happening. I'm with Adam and Kelsey. Are you okay?"

When I finished, I looked up toward the front seat and spoke. "Start talking."

"Ma'am, could I have your phone?" Adam asked, extending his hand over the seat.

My grip tightened. "No. I want to hear why you don't trust CJ."

"Has CJ had access to your phone?"

"Yes."

"I need to be sure he didn't plant—"

"Why don't you trust him?" I asked again, interrupting and still holding tight to my phone.

Adam's jaw clenched and his nostrils flared. "In Cancún, we knew that CJ was Chandler Thompson. That was a strange coincidence, but with no more information about him, he seemed harmless."

"A distraction," Kelsey said, meeting my gaze in the rearview mirror.

"And your opinion has changed?" I asked.

Adam lifted a plastic bag from the floorboard. As the contents came into view, I tried to make sense of what I saw. "What is it?"

"It's the same stationery that the note with the chocolate candies was written on."

I took it from his hand and looked down, twisting the plastic bag in my hands. "It's white stationery. That's hardly a smoking gun."

"How many thirty-one-year-old men do you know who own stationery?" Kelsey asked.

I owned stationery. I knew a few people who owned stationery. No one used it often, but that didn't mean it wasn't available. "I don't know many thirty-one-year-old men."

Adam handed me his phone. "With the speed at which things went down yesterday, there was no time for Chandler to hide what we found in his apartment. We'd assume he didn't intend for us to look."

My pulse kicked up a notch as I looked down at the phone. "What am I seeing?"

"He has a folder hidden on his computer filled with information about you."

"What kind of information?"

"There are your daily schedules going back to two months before Cancún," Kelsey said.

"How would he get that?"

"Our people are checking, but we believe he tapped into Montgomery Holdings Security's cloud."

"You've told me it's secure."

"It is. We thought it was," Adam said. "Mr. Thompson is very adept when it comes to computers and technology. It isn't a leap to believe he could hack into our system."

My mind swirled with dates and places. "Two months before Cancún?"

"It coincides with your first interest in Architech."

"But the break-in was before that."

Kelsey and Adam nodded. Finally, Kelsey answered, "We're still working on that."

"We'll know more after Mathew questions Mr. Thompson."

The private airport came into view. "Wait, are we leaving Austin?"

"Yes, ma'am," Adam replied.

"Did you send for another Montgomery plane? I don't want to rent a plane," I added, unsure what to believe.

"Mr. Sherman sent a plane."

"Van? What does he know?"

"You'll need to talk to Mr. Wilde about that."

Chapter Thirty-Four

CJ

"What the hell?" I said as a man I didn't know wearing a suit stepped in my way, stopping me from following Lena.

"Mr. Thompson, we have some questions for you."

I pushed forward, determined to catch up to Lena and Adam.

"Sir," a second man in a suit said, stepping from my apartment building, the same place where Lena had disappeared.

"Where the fuck is Lena?"

"Ms. Montgomery is in our custody now. She's with people who are determined to keep her safe."

"Your custody? Who the fuck are you? And I'm determined to keep her safe."

"Sir, come with us up to your apartment."

"Is Lena there?"

Neither man answered as I was sandwiched between them. I sized one up and the other. I could take one of them in a fair fight, two, I wasn't confident. I had the gun from my glove compartment tucked in the waist band of my shorts, but I wasn't completely prepared to use it, not to protect myself.

Lena, yes.

"Fine," I said. Taking the stairs, we traveled up to the second floor. Once to my door, the first man opened it. Inside, my apartment was in shambles.

My fists balled at my sides. "What the fuck?"

"Is this your computer in here?" the second man asked, walking down the hall toward my office.

Following a step behind, I entered. The desk and floor were littered with papers. My bookcase that had been filled with the succession of figurations for what became Architech was empty, the binders strewed around the room.

"Your computer?" he asked again.

The screen was lit. From what I could see, the computer was still working. "Yes. How did you get past my security code?"

It wasn't as if I used my birthday or the date

Architech became incorporated. It was a random sequence of numbers and letters, ones I'd memorized.

The man moved my mouse through a maze of firewalls. At first, I was familiar with what I was seeing, but then he entered a corner of cyberspace I'd never seen before.

"What can you tell us about this folder?" he asked.

"Nothing. It's not familiar."

Man number one clicked on the folder, revealing a long list of files—some documents, PDFs, JPEGs, and Excel sheets. I could only differentiate by the file names.

The second man gestured toward the desk chair. "Have a seat, Mr. Thompson. We'd like to find out how you accessed Montgomery Holdings' cloud."

"I didn't." I probably could, but I didn't.

"Sit."

"Where is Lena? Where did they take her?"

"Ms. Montgomery would prefer to avoid the publicity that comes with involving the various legal agencies. The Computer Fraud and Abuse Act makes accessing information illegally a crime, up to a class D felony, punishable by up to five years in prison."

Sitting, I looked up at the screen. The algorithm before me was running too fast to make out the sequencing of numbers. Yet as the man spoke, I watched the recursive relation, knowing I hadn't set this algorithm into play. It was a Fibonacci sequence. In essence, each number was the sum of the two preceding it.

We'd tried using that sequence with Architech early on and found there to be too many glitches. While the golden ratio was close, it wasn't precise. I'd never use Fibonacci numbers to do what these men were accusing me of.

I sat back, feeling my phone vibrate. With the two sets of eyes on me, I couldn't look to see who messaged me. I could only hope it was Lena.

"How long did it take you to plant this on my computer?" I asked.

"Sir, we found—"

"No, you didn't," I said, standing. "Call the police or FBI, or fucking Homeland Security. Get them here. You broke into my home and planted evidence."

Man number one took a step closer. "Stop harassing Ms. Montgomery. Admit that you've been stalking her. We found the stationery. If we pursue it with the authorities, you're looking at more than computer hacking. Attempted murder. Endangerment of sea life. Agree to leave her alone and we can keep this between us."

I shook my head. "I'd never do what you're accusing me of doing."

"The folder on your computer shows you've been watching her activity for over two months. Your suite in Cancún was booked immediately after hers. Was it your intention to get to know Ms. Montgomery in Cancún or to kill her?"

It was true I'd booked my Cancún stay at the last minute but not because I knew Lena would be there.

"You're fucking nuts," I said, standing and taking a step back.

"Sir, Ms. Montgomery is being presented with this evidence as we speak. She is leaving Austin and wants no further contact from you. A restraining order is in the works."

"I didn't do this." My voice was louder than necessary. "Someone wants to hurt Lena. It's not me. If you pretend it is and waste time with me, the real stalker could get to her."

Man number two looked down at his phone and lifted the screen. "Is this you?"

It was a grainy black and white picture, presumably taken from security footage of a person near a plane. I couldn't tell if it was me from the photo, but I knew it wasn't. I hadn't been near any planes since arriving home from Cancún. "No."

"And you're certain?"

"Yes. When was it taken?"

"Late yesterday morning."

"I was at Architech until I left with Lena. You can ask my brother. Check the security footage."

Man number two closed the door to my office, leaving the three of us inside the chaos. "Get comfortable, Mr. Thompson. We have more questions."

Meeting man number two at the door, I stood a few inches taller. "Get the fuck out of my apartment."

"You're not in charge, Mr. Thompson."

Pulling my gun from my waistband at my back, I pointed it at man number two and took a step back, letting man number one see what I had. "The fuck I'm not."

Man number one also had his gun drawn.

"You're going to have to shoot me or get the fuck out of my way. I can shoot both of you. You're in my home. You've ransacked my apartment. Castle Doctrine. Under Texas law, I'm justified." I pointed the barrel at the man in front of the door. "You're dead." I tilted my head toward his friend. "He may shoot me, but not before you're gone."

Number two's Adam's apple bobbed.

"I don't know who the fuck you are," I said, "but if your job is to protect Lena Montgomery, get the fuck out of my way. You know I'm not guilty, or you're both idiots and don't belong on her security team. If you're not with her team, then you could work for her stalker." The pieces seemed to be snapping into place. I wasn't certain if like the Fibonacci sequence, my train of thought was realistic or a glitch, but I went with it. "In that case, I should pull the trigger."

The man at the door stepped to the side and turning the knob, opened the door. Keeping my back toward the hallway, I continued my hold of the pistol. "Tell whoever you work for that I won't stop until Lena is safe."

Without thought for my apartment or any of the disaster inside, I took off running toward my car. Slipping the pistol back in the glove compartment, I started the Range Rover as I looked at my phone. I had multiple messages. The only one I cared about was the text from Lena.

"I'm not sure what is happening. I'm with Adam and Kelsey. Are you okay?"

Chapter Thirty-Five

Lena

"What did you tell Van?" I asked Jeremy, calling him once I was on the Sherman Corporation jet. It was a little smaller than my plane, and I knew from experience it was the jet Van used. While Archie stayed with my plane in Austin, a pilot named Ruth was flying this plane.

Jeremy's voice came through the phone. "I told him that there was a problem with your plane in Austin, Texas, and you didn't want to rent."

"So, he just sent a plane?"

"Yes," Jeremy replied as if Jeremy had asked Van for a car ride, not to send a private jet from Wisconsin to Texas.

We were currently at cruising altitude with over

three hours to go before Missoula. "You didn't tell him about..." I sighed. "Everything."

"No, but that man is curious. Experience tells me that when he's curious, he doesn't give up easily."

"I should call him."

I was seated near the rear of the fuselage having told Adam and Kelsey I wanted my space. I still wasn't certain how I felt about being whisked away, and as of yet, I'd not heard back from CJ.

"Don't be mad at Adam and Kelsey."

I scoffed. "You're not here. You don't know what I'm thinking."

"I'm not there," Jeremy said, "because they convinced me that sticking with our original schedule was best to hopefully throw off anyone watching. I know you, and I know that flying away from Austin wasn't on your schedule, not after you reached out to Chandler."

I lowered my voice. "They suspect CJ."

"I heard."

"They're wrong."

"Sometimes the heart shields what our eyes should see."

Shaking my head, I said, "No. If CJ wanted to harm me, he could have last night. I don't know who is setting CJ up, but someone is. Someone is making him look guilty." I lifted my gaze up toward my security and Liz and spoke low. "Will you do me a favor?"

"Anything."

"I'm going to call Van. After I talk to him, I'm going to let him know you want to speak to him."

"Lena, what is your devious mind coming up with?"

"I'm not alone." I covered my lips as I spoke. "And I'm not sure who I can trust. Once Julia came on the scene, Van hired a full crew of security, not the ones from Sherman Corporation. These are people he trusts with his wife and kid."

"You want to borrow them?"

"Yes. Don't tell anyone from my team. Ask Van to send them to Missoula as soon as possible."

"Honey, you're scaring me."

"Yeah, I'm fucking terrified. I'm going to call Van now."

"Hurry up. If he hurries, he could get people to Missoula not long after you land."

"I know."

Disconnecting the call, I searched for a text or message from CJ. With each passing minute, I worried about Mathew and what he was asking CJ. A sane woman would probably be thinking about the evidence Adam showed me—the stationery and the hidden folder of information straight from Montgomery Holdings.

It was official: I wasn't sane.

Maybe I had been at one time, but those days were long gone.

Searching my contacts, I called Donovan Sherman's private cell phone.

"I was hoping you'd call," Van said in the way of a greeting. There was the sound of commotion in the background before it got quiet. "Sorry. Noise is a common commodity around here. Julia says hi."

"Thank you for the jet."

His voice deepened with concern. "Talk to me, Lena. What's happening?"

"I really don't have time to give you all the details."

"Tell me you're safe. You have security."

"I do."

"This doesn't seem like a good time to tell you that I'm pissed you didn't talk to me about Architech."

"No, I'd rather reduce the number of people who hate me at the moment." With everything happening my next question came out of the blue. Maybe I wanted those within range to believe I was simply talking to an old friend. "How did you know? Julia, how did you know she was the one?"

"That seems like an out-of-the-blue question."

"You knew. I remember you telling me New Year's Eve in Chicago. You said she was special." I'd teased him about her age. In hindsight that could come back to bite me. However, CJ was older than Julia, I had that going for me.

"I can't describe it," Van answered. "I can tell you that I never doubted it. You, Liv, others thought I was crazy, but I knew. It's a feeling in my gut. I never wavered, neither did she. Why?"

I understood what he was saying. I should be doubting CJ, but I wasn't. With confidence that went to my bones, I knew he was innocent. No, he was guilty, but it wasn't because he'd stalked me. CJ was guilty of demolishing the walls around my heart, the ones I'd held sturdy for so long. In his presence, not only had they cracked, but they'd also been obliterated. Not even dust remained.

A smile graced my lips. "I think I know now, too."

"Fuck, Lena, that's the best news. Who is the lucky or unlucky man or woman?"

"Man and probably unlucky."

"No," he reassured me.

I spoke truthfully. "I'm afraid it's too late, but as my best friend, you should know that I found it... the it."

"It's not too late. Trust me."

I looked up, seeing Kelsey's and Adam's gaze coming my direction.

"Jeremy," I said into the phone, "told me you tried to steal him away."

"I'm looking for someone to share the load."

Nodding, I went on, "He has some info on a new lead. He's going to call. I hope you two can work it out."

"If you're trying to make up for keeping me out of the loop on Architech, the jury's out. I'll give him an ear."

"Thank you, Van."

"Lena, you're worrying me. You sound...different."

"Jeremy has the details." I disconnected the call.

Still no message from CJ.

Taking a deep breath, I lifted my chin toward Liz. Soon she was at my side.

"Ms. Montgomery."

"Is there food on this plane?" My coffee and yogurt from earlier were wearing off.

"Yes, ma'am. What would you like?"

"Surprise me."

As Liz stepped away, Kelsey came back and took the seat across from me.

"I'm not in a talkative mood," I said, meeting her gaze.

"I'm sorry," she said. "I'm sorry we didn't know sooner. I assumed once you learned his identity, you wouldn't..." She didn't complete her sentence, but by the expression staring my direction, Kelsey knew my feelings. I'd fallen for CJ, rule or no rule.

"He's not guilty," I said matter-of-factly. "I see the evidence. I don't believe it. Who had the access to plant it?"

Her eyes opened wide. "No one other than Montgomery security was involved."

"I'm aware."

She lowered her tone. "You know we would stop at nothing to protect you."

"Kelsey, who sent the tweet on CJ's Twitter account?"

"We can assume that it was CJ."

"Stop fucking assuming. Stop taking everything at face value. Someone is fucking with me and now with you, all of you." With each phrase the conviction in my voice grew stronger. "CJ isn't the guilty party. Get your thumbs out of your asses and figure it out because if you decide you have this settled, I'm going to be dead soon. I've decided that scenario doesn't work for my schedule. So do something, now."

"Ma'am."

As Liz arrived with iced tea and a sandwich, I

looked at Kelsey. "Don't bring me another theory on CJ, and don't stop searching until you have something to bring me."

She nodded.

Before taking a bite of the sandwich, I called my assistant back at Montgomery Holdings and told her to send me reconciliation reports on all transactions under the Montgomery umbrella over the last twenty-four months and to do it yesterday. Maybe CJ's *Law and Order* training was onto something.

Chapter Thirty-Six

CJ

"I'm not sure what is happening. I'm with Adam and Kelsey. Are you okay?"

"Where are you?"

I texted back before pulling my Range Rover away from my apartment. Pounding the steering wheel, I tried to regroup, to figure out how the last hour had gotten so fucked. There was one number I had, one person who might be able to help me.

Pushing the button on the steering wheel, I gave a voice command, "Call Jeremy Wilde."

"Calling Jeremy Wilde."

I turned right and then left, unsure where I could go. My apartment wasn't an option and neither was Architech. While watching my rearview mirror to see if I was being followed, I made my way toward Colton and Devon's current house.

"Chandler," Jeremy said, his voice coming through the speakers of my vehicle.

"Where is she?"

The moment of hesitation told me that Jeremy had been handed the same bullshit about me. Without him asking, I replied, "I would never hurt Lena. The accusations are bogus. I'd never run a Fibonacci sequence."

Jeremy laughed. "Does Lena know you're such a geek?" Before I could reply, he said, "She believes you."

I let out a breath. "She doesn't believe them?"

"No. As for me, I'm not sure."

"Fuck, Jeremy. I didn't know Lena was Lena Montgomery until you two walked in the boardroom. Yesterday, she reached out to me."

"Yeah," he said, "that's what she told me."

"Where is she? I'm fucking terrified that I'm not at her side. Some asshole wants to hurt her, and her fucking security thinks it's me, or shit, maybe the goons that stopped me from going with her are working for the stalker."

"What goons?"

"I didn't get their names. Two suits with a gun."

"Shit," he said. "How did you get away?"

"It's Texas. My gun was bigger." Or maybe I was more desperate to consider using it.

"She's on her way to Missoula," he said.

"Did they get her plane cleaned?" I asked as I changed directions and headed toward the airport.

"No. A friend sent another plane."

This was nuts. Lena had a friend who could send planes, and I was detained by assholes. "Who is this friend?"

"He knows what's happening," Jeremy said. "He's sending help too."

"What kind of help?"

Jeremy's voice deepened. "Chandler, if you're sincere about Lena, get to Missoula as fast as you can."

"I'm on my way to the airport."

"No airline flies nonstop. Give me a second."

"Okay," I muttered, wondering what Jeremy was thinking as I made my way south.

A little over a minute later, Jeremy was back on the call. "Go to Executive Airport in Pflugerville. The Montgomery Holdings jet is still there. I just spoke to Archie Evans, our pilot. The fish smell isn't completely gone, but he said it's bearable."

The small hairs on my arms stood to attention.

"He'll fly me to Missoula?" Memories of the goons came back. "I want to trust you. Tell me I won't be flown to parts unknown."

"He'll bring you here. Archie agreed to keep his passenger list to himself."

Does that mean Archie isn't telling the security?

Is Jeremy second-guessing the security team too?

"I love her," I said. "She's not dying on my watch."

"I believe you," Jeremy replied. "Does she know how you feel?"

"I haven't told her, but I sure as fuck hope she knows."

"Get to Missoula and tell her."

"On my way." I disconnected our call and did a U-turn.

The Executive Airport used to be known as the Bird's Nest. I'd been there once to meet with an investor from out of state. Numbers weren't my only specialty. I had what some people called a photographic memory. No GPS needed as I headed north on 130.

A text message notification came up on the screen. 'Text message from Lena.' I hit the icon to have it read to me.

"Are you okay? What did Mathew do?"

Who the fuck was Mathew?

I could only assume that was one of the suits, Tweedle Dee or Tweedle Dum.

I pressed the voice response and spoke, "I love you, Lena. I didn't say it when I should have. I want you to know. Mathew didn't give me his name. I'm coming for you. I promised to be at your side, and no one is going to stop me. Stay safe. At this point, I don't trust anyone but you and me."

Chapter Thirty-Seven

Lena

Jeremy's message had been short and sweet, telling me that Van was interested in the proposition. Speaking in codes was apparently my new form of communication. As I looked up from my laptop, I questioned the people around me. I'd trusted Adam and Kelsey with my life, and yet I wondered about what CJ said about Adam. If it were true, if Adam wanted more than our business relationship, he had never given me any indication. Or I hadn't picked up on it.

Maybe it was simply a testosterone thing between him and CJ.

I tried to think back to my last relationship. As names and faces came to mind, I realized that there wasn't one that stood out, not like CJ. I'd told CJ the truth about my past. By definition, as an employee of Infidelity, I'd sold myself—my body and my companionship.

I was a prostitute, but not a whore.

The line might seem blurred to some, but it wasn't. I sold an available commodity that I had to support Madison and myself. Who I slept with from that time on was always on my terms. I also had no problem satisfying my own needs. There was no shame in either avenue.

The phone to the side of my laptop lit up.

Seeing CJ's name upon the screen flooded my system with relief. His message wasn't a text but a voice mail. Taking off my noise-canceling earphones, I took my phone into the bathroom of the plane.

After securing the door, I hit the arrow and listened to CJ's message. The timbre of his deep voice resonated through me, but it was his words that made me pause.

"I love you, Lena. I didn't say it when I should have. I want you to know."

I moved the small circle backward and played that part of the message again and again. "I love you too," I whispered aloud. Deep in my heart I knew it to be true. Finally, after the third or fourth time, I let the message continue to play. CJ was coming to me. That same heart that he'd somehow found, the one I'd hidden behind years of war wounds, scars, and ice, leaped and simultaneously sank.

There was nothing I longed for more than to be in his arms and at the same time, if CJ stayed in Austin, away from me, he would be safe. I still didn't know what had gone down with Mathew, but judging from CJ's message, he had gotten away.

I sent a text message back.

"Please stay in Austin. I don't want you in danger."

I waited for a response, not wanting to play an audible message with an audience.

The icon lit up. Another voice message. "I didn't take the job. You're not my boss."

His response made me smile. I sent one more message.

"I think I love you, too."

"Tell me in person."

. . .

I nodded. It was what I wanted to do.

There was a knock on the bathroom door.

"Ms. Montgomery, are you all right?"

Gritting my teeth, I flushed the toilet and ran water in the sink. When I opened the door, Kelsey was waiting. "I'm on a fucking plane."

"Ma'am, I'd like to check your phone."

"For what?"

"You didn't give it to Adam earlier. If CJ had access, he could have installed a tracking app."

"He didn't." I held tight to my phone. "Do you have any new ideas?"

"Not yet. We've been in contact with security in Missoula. Your house is secure. No one has approached it or the Montgomery offices."

Closing my eyes, I nodded.

"You should rest," she suggested.

"Have Liz bring me more tea. I have work to do." I feigned a smile as I slipped my phone under the neckline of my blouse and into the edge of my bra. "Don't bother me unless you have news."

This was me being me. I could do it, slip into the mode and move on as if my life wasn't in danger and the walls around my heart hadn't been incinerated by the most unlikely of men.

My thoughts filled with numbers and mergers as I

looked through the reports from Gigi. In the last two years, Montgomery Holdings had made multiple acquisitions, the most recent was Architech. There were stock buy-ins and buyouts. A smile flirted on my lips at the name Wade Pharmaceuticals. The last report I'd read said the small company was still going strong. The coalition of pharmaceutical companies that Julia Sherman proposed was effective in boosting their lobbying power. Their refocus on generic insulin was keeping them afloat.

My smile faded as I recalled seeing Logan Butler at a board meeting for Wade. I'd been the largest share-holder at the time and his presence proved he was involved with a SPAC that had been trying to use Wade as a bargaining chip.

Closing my eyes, I recalled the expression on Logan's face as he listened to my speech to the share-holders. I remembered the satisfaction I felt, knowing I'd accomplished more than either he or his brother. Logan knew it. He knew my dirtiest secret, and he knew that I had the ability to bring him down.

I hadn't.

Instead, I was like a cat playing with my dinner.

Slowly demolishing his world.

Reveling in his troubles.

Behind the scenes, I've had my hand in making his

and his brother's lives more difficult. The whole SEC thing. I'd also been the one to secure his nephew's employment. That had been for Van's wife more than the nephew.

My gut was right when it came to business.

I needed to think about my stalker as I would business.

It was Logan.

Somehow, he was behind this.

He didn't simply dislike me. The venom in his stare at that meeting was as strong as it had been the night Van left him bloodied and took me away before I could pull the trigger.

Taking off my earphones, I motioned to Adam and Kelsey. Soon they were both seated across the table from me. "My gut tells me it's Logan. The thing about Madison and Missoula was intentional."

Adam removed his phone from the pocket of his suit coat and looked at Kelsey.

"What?" she asked.

"Where's your phone?"

"Over there," she said, lifting her chin toward the seat where she'd been.

"What is it?" I asked.

Adam's blue stare met mine after he read his screen. "If it's Logan Butler, he's not working alone."

My eyes widened. "What did you learn?"

"The envelope with the candy...the glue was tested for trace saliva. Currently, the only thing they know for sure is that the DNA is female with biomarkers for Sjögren's syndrome."

Female.

I collapsed against the seat. "A woman." Sjögren's syndrome was an immune system disorder that attacked the healthy cells that produce saliva and tears. "Isn't that syndrome mostly in older women?"

Adam and Kelsey shrugged.

My thoughts focused on women I'd wronged. The world of high finance was male-dominated. A new idea came to me as I watched the nonverbal exchange between my bodyguards. "It wasn't CJ."

Adam shook his head. "Same as Logan. He could be working with a woman."

My fist pounded the table, making my phone jump and the tea in my glass slosh. "It is not CJ," I said emphatically. With two sets of eyes on me, I lowered my tone. "Can they determine the person who licked the envelope?"

"It takes time and depends on the sample size and if the person is in the federal registry," Kelsey explained.

"Gwen."

Adam and Kelsey sat straighter.

"Gwen Butler?" Adam asked with a nod. "She and her husband Marlin are sweating the SEC."

"Right," I said. "Stop fucking around with the theory that CJ is involved. Find out where Gwen and Marlin Butler have been for the last three months."

Both of my bodyguards stood. As Kelsey walked away, Adam remained.

"Talk," I said.

"Who is Michael Ricks?"

"I don't know," I answered honestly.

Adam's jaw clenched and his nostrils flared. "He's an hour away from Missoula with a few of his team."

Van.

I smiled. "Van sent them."

"Are you firing us?"

"Not if you're innocent," I said, repeating what Adam had said about CJ.

"What the fuck, Lena?" Adam growled.

"Ms. Montgomery," I corrected. "I told you to get your thumbs out of your asses, and I meant it. I'm a little busy for the next fifty years to end up dead before my ninety-third birthday."

"And who has been at your side, keeping you safe?"

"You," I admitted. "And Kelsey, the whole team. That shit you pulled in Austin, whisking me away and not listening to me about CJ." I stood, meeting Adam in the aisle. We had the attention of Liz and Kelsey. "I'm still in charge, Adam. Van sent his trusted people to help. Either they'll help or they'll run the show. You decide if you're still on my team."

"I run this team and that isn't changing."

"You'll work with Mr. Ricks. Someone told me that fresh eyes were valuable. Mr. Ricks and his team are fresh eyes."

Adam's head was shaking, but his lips were sealed. At the moment, that was wise.

"Are we clear?" I asked.

"Yes, Ms. Montgomery. We're clear."

"Oh, and CJ is coming to Missoula." Before Adam could comment, I added, "And he's staying with me. You can post people outside and keep the cameras and alarms. Kelsey will no longer be necessary."

Adam stood taller. "Do you know when he'll arrive?"

"No. I don't know what airline he's flying, but when he arrives, he's allowed entry. No more BS."

Chapter Thirty-Eight

CJ

As we traveled northwest, I stared helplessly at the tops of clouds, wishing I'd been more prepared—a laptop, a change of clothes, anything. When I'd first entered Lena's plane, I'd detected the lingering stench of fish. Now, as the wheels landed on the tarmac, I didn't notice it. That probably meant I'd grown accustomed and needed a shower.

Three-and-a-half hours was a long time to sit and think.

I'd come to a few conclusions and constructed a list of questions. Thankfully, I'd found a tablet and pen in one of the cupboards. One recurring thought was of the picture Tweedle Dee or Tweedle Dum showed me. I hadn't looked at it long enough to remember every detail, but what I could remember was a grainy image of a person in a sweatshirt hoodie. The Executive Airport wasn't without security. The planes I'd seen when I arrived came in all sizes and no doubt with hefty price tags. No random person would be able to get to Lena's plane. There was something else. Other than the person, there was nothing—no container of fish. According to the pilot, the fish had been in a container that resembled other containers in the luggage hold, those filled with supplies.

Could it have been there since before they left Missoula?

"Mr. Thompson," Mr. Evans said, coming from the cockpit. "Mr. Wilde sent a car for you."

"A car."

I fucking hoped it wasn't being driven by Adam or the Tweedle twins.

Releasing the seal on the door allowed a rush of fresh air to enter the plane. I looked around the cabin, knowing I had nothing but the clothes on my back and my list in the pocket of my shorts. I was hardly dressed for a private aircraft. "Thank you again for the ride."

The stairs lowered as Mr. Evans nodded. "I had to fly back, so I'm happy it worked out."

Standing at the top of the stairs, I looked around at

the mountains in the distance. "This isn't a private airport?"

"No, sir. This is the private runway of the international airport."

"Where is this plane stored?" I asked.

"We have a hangar over that way."

"May I see it?"

The pilot nodded. "You will. It's where the car is waiting. If you want a quick tour..."

"I do."

As we walked across the pavement, Mr. Evans explained the process of the tugs that move the planes from one place to the other. Montgomery Holdings had multiple business jets. Lena mostly flew the one we were in.

"Is the luggage hold temperature controlled?"

"No, it's pressurized," Archie said. "These planes are different from commercial airplanes. The temperature can get very cold during flight."

"That makes sense," I said, "considering the air temperature at high altitudes."

"You don't want to ride in there. Frostbite" —he shrugged— "if you don't succumb to hypothermia first."

The large door of the hangar was open, and Mr. Evans waved at a man driving one of the tugs. "He'll be back with the plane," he explained.

Beside the waiting car, there were two other jets with the same MH monogram on the side. Their doors were closed. There was also another plane with Sherman written on the side.

"This building is huge."

"As you can see, we can fit additional planes." He pointed at the Sherman plane. "Mr. Sherman sent that one for Ms. Montgomery to fly home."

"Sherman?"

"Donovan Sherman."

Now that was a name I'd heard before.

I peered at the walls and ceiling, spotting multiple security cameras. "The planes stay in here. I assume it's secure. Who sees the security footage?"

"Oh yes, it's secure. Most of the cameras belong to Montgomery Holdings. There's one in each hangar that belongs to the airport. They don't want anything to happen to the private planes either. Looks bad for business and the astronomical monthly rental charge."

The driver of the waiting car opened the back door and Jeremy Wilde got out.

"Chandler."

A smile came to my face at the sight of a familiar face. "Jeremy, I didn't know you'd be here."

"Lena asked me to make sure you had a direct trip to her house."

"Yeah, there was an issue earlier."

"So you mentioned. I can fill you in on what's happening."

I offered the pilot my hand. "Thank you, Mr. Evans, for the trip and the tour."

"Mr. Thompson."

Settling into the back seat with Jeremy, the driver drove us out of the hangar moments before the plane I'd been flying in was tugged toward us.

Jeremy's nose scrunched. "Fish."

"Yes." I lifted my t-shirt to my nose. I was still wearing the softball clothes from this morning. "I could use a change of clothes."

"I see you traveled light."

"There was the slight issue with my apartment being ransacked and two suits who weren't going to let me leave."

His eyes opened wide. "I didn't know about the ransack."

"Lena is safe?"

For the next ten to fifteen minutes, Jeremy filled me in on recent happenings. DNA tests on the envelope's glue indicated it had been sealed with female saliva. He also told me about Donovan Sherman. Not only had Mr. Sherman sent his plane, he'd also sent a few of his trusted security team.

"Does that mean Lena is suspicious of Adam and Kelsey—her own team?"

Jeremy shrugged. "Honestly, she's probably suspicious of me. Right now, I think the only person she trusts is you." He narrowed his gaze. "If that's misplaced, you'll regret it."

"It's not, but I think the culprit is closer to her than she realizes."

"What makes you think that?"

"Did you know that the luggage hold is pressurized but not temperature controlled? Mr. Evans said it gets very cold."

"I haven't given it thought."

"I have," I said. "What if the fish were put in there before you took off for Austin? Think about it. They wouldn't be detected until the plane sat in the hangar. Then when it was moved outside, the temperature must have skyrocketed. No one gets into the plane to move it. They have those tugs. Therefore, if the smell was starting to infiltrate the cabin, no one would have known."

"Montgomery security would have been notified if someone entered the hangar here."

"Unless that someone was supposed to be there."

"I'll have Adam look at the footage."

"I want to look at it and not the footage from the

Montgomery cameras, the one from the Missoula Airport camera."

"You don't trust Adam."

Jeremy didn't ask, but I shrugged and said, "I trust Lena, and maybe you."

The car approached a white iron gate with two large brick columns on either side. The car slowed and the gate opened. The long driveway was surrounded by a lush green yard. "How much land does Lena have?"

"A little over ten acres."

"How did someone get inside her house?"

"Adam's upped the cameras since then. The culprit cut the power to the house, rendering the security useless. When it was turned back on, that's when the fish tank fried."

I shook my head. "Backup generator."

"Yes, sir, she has that now."

The excessively large light-brick house came into view. A second gate lowered into the pavement as we approached a circular driveway complete with a fountain. The driver pulled up to the front door. I turned to Jeremy. "Are you coming in?"

He shook his head. "I've been in. Lena's in a mood." He grinned. "I wish you luck."

"As long as her security doesn't shoot me, I think I'll be fine."

"I like your positivity. She needs it."

As I got out of the car, the front door opened, and Lena's smile took my breath away. She waved to Jeremy as the car pulled away. Taking her in my arms, I pulled her close until my lips met hers.

"I missed you," she said, ushering me inside.

I stood in awe as I took in her home, the massive two-story foyer with the large staircase leading up to the second level. Above me was a giant chandelier hanging from a glass dome filled with mirrors and reflecting the light. "I'm glad I didn't take you to my apartment."

Chapter Thirty-Nine

Lena

"It's just a house," I said, securing the front door. When I turned, CJ was staring at the various pieces of art. "Is that a Van Gogh?"

"Yes." I shrugged. "I think my art collection is my way of feeling closer to my sister." I pointed to a framed piece over the staircase. "That's Madison's work."

"She's talented."

I nodded. "This piece was from years ago. Since then..." I wrapped my arms around my midsection. "She's been diagnosed as bipolar with psychotic features. Hallucinations or delusions," I explained.

"And you're helping her get help."

"I'm trying. It's not easy with her in prison."

"I'd like to meet her."

A lump formed in my throat. "You would?"

CJ reached for my hand. "Yes, Lena. She's important to you. Of course, I want to meet her."

As he stood closer, I scrunched my nose. "Jeremy told me that he got you on my plane. I can tell the fish smell isn't gone."

CJ smiled. "A shower would be nice." He reached for my hand. "Now that I'm with you again and know you're all right."

"I'm not, but I'm better with you here."

"You don't happen to have some men's clothes in this giant house, do you?"

It was then I realized CJ didn't have any luggage. "No, but I can get some." I grinned. "Or we could go with plan B."

His turquoise stare shimmered. "You know I'm a fan of having a backup plan." He looked around the adjoining rooms. "You have a lot of windows."

"I also have a bit of land. No one can see inside."

I tugged on his hand. "Come upstairs. I'll show you the shower and call for some clothes."

Once on the second level, I led CJ toward the master bedroom suite.

"This is a lot of house for one person."

"There are other bedrooms."

He stopped at the threshold of my bedroom and

cupped my cheeks. "I'm willing to share." His lips brushed mine.

Despite the fish aroma, I melded against his chest. As his arms surrounded me and the beating of his heart sounded in my ear, I sighed and wrapped my arms around his torso. When I looked up, his gaze was on me. "Thank you for getting here as soon as you could."

"I never intended for us to be separated."

I took a step back. "Oh, what happened with Mathew?"

CJ scoffed. "Is that Tweedle Dee or Tweedle Dum?"

"There were two?" I asked. "I only saw one."

He ran his thumb over my cheek. "None of that is important. I'm here now. You're not getting rid of me."

"I don't want you to be in danger."

"Lena, I won't leave your side." His grin grew. "With the exception of a shower."

I tilted my head toward the bathroom. "Make yourself at home. Towels are in the cupboard. And I'll call Kelsey. She can run and get you some clothes until you have a chance to shop tomorrow."

As CJ walked toward the shower, I remembered that members of my security stayed out at the pool house. Maybe there were some men's clothes in there.

"You can join me," CJ called from the bathroom as

the sound of water told me that he'd turned on the shower.

Going to the bathroom door, I pushed it inward in time to see his round ass, the V in his lower back, and wide shoulders. The tattoos on his arms reminded me of the waves in Mexico. His hair hung loose as he stepped under the warm water.

"I could get used to the view," I said.

His handsome smile turned my way through the glass. "Good. The view from this side is stunning."

"Hardly." My skirt and blouse that I'd worn for two days was in the hamper, and I was currently wearing a gray tennis skort and light blue tank top.

CJ opened the shower door. "You're a beautiful woman, Lena. You don't get to negotiate that fact."

"Let me throw these in the washer," I said, picking up his clothes. "And I'll find you something. In the meantime, I know how sexy you are in a towel."

"You've had this planned," he said with a laugh. "Ever since that first breakfast when you said you'd like me without clothes."

"You're right. It's all part of my master plan."

That breakfast was nearly a month ago, and somehow it felt longer as if I'd known CJ for a lifetime. Simply in his presence I was lighter. I could put away *the* Lena Montgomery and live in the moment.

Leaving CJ in the shower, I considered who could go shopping. Adam was with Michael Ricks. Mr. Ricks met us in the hangar and introduced himself and those with him. I'd called Van once I was home and offered him my thanks again. He'd told me that he trusts Michael implicitly, and he could stay as long as necessary.

I hoped it wouldn't be that long.

After tossing CJ's clothes in the washing machine, I called Kelsey. "Can you go to someplace in town and pick up some clothes for CJ?"

"Yes?"

"He literally arrived with the clothes on his back, and since he flew here with Archie, there's a little problem of a fish aroma."

"He flew with Archie?"

"Yes, Jeremy arranged it."

"We weren't notified."

"Kelsey, the clothes. Shorts and shirts are fine. He can go shopping tomorrow."

"How long is CJ staying?" she asked.

I never want him to leave.

I didn't say that. Instead, I replied, "As long as he wants. Please hurry."

I disconnected the call and walked down the stairs, past the main floor, to the lower level. This floor was only visible from the back of the house. Beyond the glass doors were the pool and pool house. My land behind was flat and went on for acres. Since the first break-in, the number of surveillance cameras had increased. No one other than groundskeepers should be there.

Purple and crimson hues settled near the mountains as the sun fell lower in the evening sky. Opening the door, I lifted my face to the sky, enjoying the summer air that was not as stifling as in Texas. I stepped onto the pool deck as lights illuminated in the water, changing colors. A few feet away, the pool house door opened from within. The small hairs on my arms stood to attention.

My panic subsided as Kelsey came out, carrying a pink bag and juggling her large refillable water bottle.

"I didn't know you were here," I said, letting out a breath.

"I was getting a few things to take home," she said, patting the cloth bag.

"You were staying in the big house."

"Adam said Ricks and his men would be staying out here. I figured they didn't need feminine hygiene supplies or my trusted insulated bottle."

I shook my head. "I was coming out to see if there were any clothes that CJ could borrow."

Kelsey shut the door. "No, it's all cleaned out for Sherman's men."

"All three of them?" I asked, thinking the pool house wasn't that large. It had one bedroom, a living room, and a kitchenette.

"I think they're going to be taking turns." She shrugged. "Adam's in charge. Or at least he thinks he is."

"Tomorrow, I want to be briefed on everything."

Kelsey lifted her car keys. "I'll go on that errand now. The gates are being monitored."

"Okay." I turned to go back inside as Kelsey took the sidewalk around the outside of the main house. The room where Kelsey had slept was in this lower level. Going to that bedroom, I searched the dresser drawers and closet. All her things were gone.

I couldn't explain what felt wrong, but something did.

Going back outside, I looked from side to side before trying the pool house door. The knob didn't budge. "Locked," I muttered.

Though I rarely went out to it, I was most certain I had a key upstairs. Once back inside, I heard my name. Going up the stairs to the main level, I found CJ in the kitchen with a white towel around his hips. Stopping at the top step, I couldn't hide my grin.

CJ's wide chest was still tanned from Cancún with just the right amount of dark hair that trailed down his tight stomach, disappearing under the towel. His chin-length hair was damp and combed back.

"I should tell Kelsey to forget the shopping trip."

"Are we alone?" he asked with a grin.

"If I say yes..."

"I can lose the towel."

In two long strides he met me at the top of the stairs. Craning my neck upward, I took in the clean scent of my eucalyptus bodywash as I reached up, running my fingers through his wavy dark mane.

"I wanted to tell you something in person," I confessed, "but now I'm scared."

His hands came to my hips. "You're not scared. You're Lena Montgomery."

With my hands on his shoulders, I shook my head. "I can be scared with you, CJ. I don't want to be, but I can. It's a gift."

"I know it's too soon and there's a whole lot of shit happening, but I meant what I said. I love you."

I nodded. "It's way too soon, but since this could be my last day on this earth, I want you to know, I think I love you, too."

Tipping his forehead to mine, CJ's sexy smile grew,

complete with the dimple I was loving. "Convenient. And no more talking about your last day."

Our lips came together as I palmed his scratchy cheeks. He tasted like toothpaste. When our kiss ended, I grinned. "Did you use my toothbrush?"

"I think we had this discussion."

Warmth filled my cheeks. "Your lips, my pussy. My lips, your cock."

"That was the one."

I turned toward the large kitchen. "I have more than turkey sandwiches."

His smile quirked. "I was thinking about eating, just not food."

Chapter Forty

Lena

Waking, I reached across the bed. The space was empty. My pulse kicked up as I sat and looked around the room, my eyes adjusting to the scant moonlight coming from beyond the windows.

"CJ?" I called.

My muscles tightened and my circulation thumped in my ears. Once out of bed, I checked the bathroom. Even without turning on the lights, I knew it was empty. Inside my closet, I found my long satin robe. Securing it around me, I went on a search. My first thought was that he was in the kitchen. Our dinner had been hours ago and admittedly, we'd burned more than a few calories since then.

The house was quiet and dark as I traversed the

catwalk toward the back stairs. The two-story windows looked out on the back of the house. A bluish-green fog flashed through the black sky. There was no way to know when the aurora borealis will make its appearance. For a moment I stopped and waited for another wave. The color reminded me of the blue flames in CJ's stare when he's in the height of passion. The blue flame my mother had always said was a good omen. That was what CJ was, my blue flame, my silver lining.

Taking my eyes off the sky, I looked all the way down to the pool. My breath caught, spotting CJ outside. Wearing a pair of nylon shorts, he wasn't alone. Squinting my eyes, it appeared he was speaking to Kelsey.

This was crazy. It was three in the morning.

Hurrying, I made my way down to the lower level. Opening the glass door, I called out, "What is happening?"

CJ shot me a look, one like I hadn't seen before. He lifted his hand, and his tone was gruff. "Go back inside, Lena."

I didn't listen. "Kelsey?" I asked as I walked barefoot across the pool deck. It wasn't until I was closer that I saw the gun in her hand. "What the hell?"

"Ms. Montgomery, go inside. Mr. Ricks is on his way."

"Put the gun down," I said, stepping in front of CJ. My progress was quickly stalled as CJ pushed me aside, stepping closer to Kelsey.

"There is no one coming, is there?" CJ asked.

"We have the evidence," she said. "Once the police..."

My mind was a blur. I couldn't make sense of what was happening. The northern lights swirled. CJ leaped. Kelsey screamed as the flash and explosive bang of the gun turned the night from fright to terror.

My ears echoed with the loud shot as I knelt down to where CJ and Kelsey were on the concrete.

"Oh my God. CJ?"

Pushing the gun away, CJ held Kelsey pinned to the concrete deck.

"Call Adam or Ricks," he said.

My mind wasn't computing. Looking up at the pool house, I said, "I thought they were supposed to be here."

"He's lying," Kelsey screamed. "He was going to hurt you."

In the darkness, CJ's turquoise stare looked up at me, and I knew without a doubt, CJ wasn't the guilty party. "Can you hold her?"

"Yes. Call Adam now."

I pulled the sash from my robe and handed it to CJ. "Use this. I'll go get my phone."

"Ms. Montgomery..."

I didn't listen to Kelsey as I walked in a daze back to my room. Finding my phone on the bedside stand, I entered my code. There were three missed calls from Adam and two from Jeremy.

Hitting the icon, I called Adam.

"Lena, stay in the house."

"It's Kelsey. I don't know how it's her, but it's her."

"I'm almost there."

"CJ has her. She tried to shoot him or me..."

"Are you okay? CJ?"

I nodded. "Hurry."

Rushing back to the catwalk, I could see CJ had Kelsey's hands tied behind her. As I walked, I called Jeremy.

"I'm sorry," I began, ready to apologize for the time.

"Honey," he interrupted. "I'm at the gate. My pass isn't working. Adam just got here too." There was commotion in the background before Jeremy said, "Adam got the gate open. The police are right behind us. We're all coming."

"Why?" I asked, swallowing my emotions. "Why are you all coming?"

"Kelsey..."

"How did you know?"

"Chandler," Jeremy said.

"He called you?"

"We're passing the second gate."

"Tell Adam to go around to the pool."

Dropping the robe, I slipped on a pair of shorts and a top. As I came down the staircase, blue sirens filled my front windows. By the time I made it back to the pool deck, Kelsey was standing, surrounded by three uniformed police officers.

When CJ saw me, he came my way, wrapping his arm around me.

"How did you know?" I asked.

Jeremy and Adam came over to where we were standing. Jeremy looked at CJ. "I called the airport and asked about their security. The cameras reboot every seven days. They still had the footage from last Tuesday when Adam and Lena came back from New York. If we wouldn't have asked for it soon, it would have been lost."

My body trembled in CJ's grasp.

"What was seen?" CJ asked.

"Kelsey went to the hangar Wednesday morning. We can see her entering."

"The fish?" I asked.

"She drove into the hangar. The footage is fuzzy,

but yes, she's seen taking a large container from the trunk of the car and putting it in the luggage hold."

I looked at Adam. "You didn't know?"

He shook his head. "I trusted her. She was the one who reviewed our footage, telling me there was nothing."

Stepping away from the three of them, I walked to where the police had Kelsey detained. "Why?"

"You were never in real danger."

"I trusted you, Kelsey. I thought of you as a friend."

"No. You didn't. You think of yourself as better when you're not. You don't care about anyone but yourself. Not until him." She lifted her chin toward CJ. "He was the perfect scapegoat."

"Ms. Nicholson," the policeman said, beginning to lead her away.

I'd heard Kelsey's name a thousand times. I'd read it on her resume. I'd used it when I introduced her, but for the first time, I wondered. "Wait? Are you related to Avery Nicholson?"

She stood tall. "He was my father."

"Is this about..."

"My father committed suicide when I was just a child. My mother found out about his infidelity and left him. He swore it wasn't true. He was repaying a debt. The last time I saw him, he was begging my mom to forgive him. It took a lot of digging when I was older, but I found out about that company."

"You think I'm responsible?"

"Ms. Nicholson, I'd advise you to not say any more."

As they took her away, CJ reached for my hand.

"Why were you outside with her?" I asked.

"I heard a noise and saw her coming and going from the pool house."

I looked at Adam. He went to the pool house and opened the door. We all peered in around him. The pool house looked the same as it had. It even smelled piney clean.

Adam stopped. "I think we should have this place thoroughly searched. I wondered why she was concerned about Mr. Sherman's men staying here. She said it was just in need of cleaning and said she'd stay here tonight."

"What do you think she had in there?" CJ asked.

"She left with a pink bag full of things earlier in the evening, before she bought CJ's clothes." I looked over at him, his bare chest and low-hanging shorts.

"The police will check her car and apartment." Adam looked at me. "Ms. Montgomery, she passed all the background checks. Who was her father?"

That was my dirtiest secret.

I shook my head. "It sounds like he was someone that got mixed up in a mess."

"She blames you?"

CJ didn't speak. He held tight to my hand. When I looked up, I could feel and sense his compassion and understanding. This man I had only recently met knew a secret that even Adam and Jeremy didn't know.

I leaned against CJ. "I guess this means it's finally over."

He kissed the top of my head. "No, Lena. This is only the beginning."

Epilogue

CJ

Eight months later

"Hey, handsome."

Sitting in my office at Architech, a Venus subsidiary, I looked up from my desk, struck by the gorgeous woman in my doorway. "Hey, beautiful."

Lena came inside, closing the door behind her. She was in her *the* Lena mode, the air filling with the scent of Creed Royal Service, and her bright red lips curled into a sexy grin.

Leaning back against the leather chair, I smiled. "Is this visit business or pleasure?"

She trailed the tips of her finger over the expanse of my desk until she was wedged against the desk and between my knees. "I was on my way home when I decided I didn't want to wait for you to come home."

I lifted my eyebrows. "Do you have any ideas?"

"Adam dropped me off. I'm in your hands now. And your assistant has left for the day."

Tipping my head toward the large screens on my desk, I sighed. "I'm kind of working on a thing."

Her luscious chocolate stare swirled as she licked her lips and eased her arms out of the matching jacket over her dress.

"I approve of a striptease."

"I left my panties in my purse."

My cock twitched as I stood and after a quick kiss, spun her around. Pressing between her slender shoulders, I pushed her breasts to the desktop as I reached under the hem of her dress, finding her slick pussy. "You're soaked."

She craned her neck, her soft brown eyes on me. "I've been thinking about this."

Bunching her dress around her waist, I swatted one ass cheek and then the other, leaving bright red handprints. Her yelp filled the air.

"*That* was for blurring your own lines."

"You're fired," she said with a grin.

"I don't work for you. In here, I'm the boss."

After freeing myself from my jeans, I leaned down,

purposely teasing her sensitive skin of her neck with my warm breath. "Hold on tight, Ms. Montgomery. Once I'm done, I want those red lips to leave a ring around my cock."

Her breathing came fast as she nodded.

Lifting her sexy ass and spreading her legs, I buried myself in the same tight pussy I'd been in this morning and nearly every day since making Missoula my new home.

Lena's fingers blanched as she held tight to the edge of the desk. Holding her hips, I moved in and out as her core contracted. The office filled with the sounds of our bodies coming together, mingled with the curses and moans. Stars danced behind my eyelids as Lena's body trembled, and she called out my name.

Pulling out, I helped Lena spin. As I was about to kiss her lips, she dropped to her knees.

"Fuck, Lena."

I held tight to the edge of the desk as Lena took over, sucking and licking. Her red lips parted, taking me to the back of her throat. This woman on her knees was the same woman who recently licensed my hard- and software to a major hotel chain, earning more than what she'd paid for it. Architech was becoming a contender in a world she dominated.

I couldn't be more fucking proud of her.

With a sexy smile, Lena stood, her lips taking mine, sharing the sweet taste of her and the musky taste of me.

"Come home," she said as she straightened her dress. She looked at the screens. "You're a genius, remember. You can do this tomorrow."

"It will take longer than tomorrow."

"Then come home. We're leaving tomorrow night for Wisconsin."

Wisconsin.

"The judge is ruling on Madison's sentence. We should be there for her."

The lawyers had informed Lena that with the crime being taken down to a class F felony, Madison was most likely looking at a fine and monitored institutionalization. Lena had a new and better facility lined up and her checkbook ready for whatever fine the judge issued.

"And I'm finally going to get to meet your knight in shining armor," I said.

"Van and Julia will be there, but Van's not my knight." Lena brushed her lips over my cheek. "You're my silver lining. I hated what Kelsey did to me, but if that hadn't happened, we wouldn't have met."

After tucking myself away and zipping my jeans, I opened the side drawer on my desk. When I looked up,

Lena was picking up her purse. "Before we go to Wisconsin."

Lena's eyes grew wide at the blue velvet box in my hand. "CJ?"

It was my turn to fall to my knees. I opened the box, revealing a four-carat emerald-cut diamond on a platinum band. Lena's painted fingertips were at her lips as she stared down at me.

"I'm better at numbers than I am words."

Her smile grew as her eyes glistened.

"I love you, Lena Montgomery, every side of you, every inch of you. The Lena the world sees and the one you keep only for me. When I went to Cancún, I thought I'd drink in the sunshine and mourn the loss of my world. I had no way of knowing that instead, my world was about to be blown to smithereens by a seductive lioness. With you, I've found what it's like to love someone unconditionally." I looked around the office. "You not only restored my world, but made it so much more. I don't know what the future holds for us, I only know that I want to take it on, every day, with you at my side." I removed the ring from the box. "Will you marry me?"

With tears on her cheeks, Lena nodded. I eased the ring onto her fourth finger of her left hand. I stood. "I want to be your husband. You don't have to take my name. You are *the* Lena Montgomery."

She looked down at her hand, splaying her fingers and back to me. "I want your name, CJ. Montgomery Holdings will still be Montgomery. I want you to know that I want to be your wife, for you to be my husband. Maybe I'll hyphenate."

"As long as I'm at your side, nothing else matters."

AND THEY LIVED HAPPILY EVER AFTER

I hope you enjoyed SILVER LINING – a blurred-lines novel. If you did and you don't know Lena's friends Donovan and Julia Sherman, check out the Sin Series. Begin today with book one, **RED SIN**.

Be sure to start from the beginning with Aleatha's brand-new series, Royal Reflections, where things are not always as they appear. Download book one, **RUTHLESS REIGN** today.

If you'd like to learn more about the company, Infidelity, check out the INFIDELITY series, ready to binge, beginning with **BETRAYAL**.

What to do now

LEND IT: Did you enjoy SILVER LINING? Do you have a friend who'd enjoy SILVER LINING? SILVER LINING may be lent one time. Sharing is caring!

RECOMMEND IT: Do you have multiple friends who'd enjoy my dark romance with twists and turns and an all new sexy and infuriating anti-hero? Tell them about it! Call, text, post, tweet...your recommendation is the nicest gift you can give to an author!

REVIEW IT: Tell the world. Please go to the retailer where you purchased this book, as well as Goodreads, and write a review. Please share your thoughts about SILVER LINING on:

*Amazon, SILVER LINING Customer Reviews

*Barnes & Noble, SILVER LINING, Customer Reviews

*Apple Books, SILVER LINING Customer Reviews

* BookBub, SILVER LINING Customer Reviews

*Goodreads.com/Aleatha Romig

ALL AVAILABLE TO READ ON KINDLE UNLIMITED

ROYAL REFLECTIONS SERIES:

RUTHLESS REIGN

November 2022

RESILIENT REIGN

January 2023

RAVISHING REIGN

April 2023

RELEVANT REIGN

June 2023

READY TO BINGE:

SIN SERIES:

RED SIN

October 2021

GREEN ENVY

January 2022

GOLD LUST

April 2022

BLACK KNIGHT

June 2022

STAND-ALONE ROMANTIC SUSPENSE:

SILVER LINING

October 2022

KINGDOM COME

November 2021

DEVIL'S SERIES (Duet):

DEVIL'S DEAL

May 2021

ANGEL'S PROMISE

June 2021

WEB OF SIN:

SECRETS

October 2018

LIES

December 2018

PROMISES

January 2019

TANGLED WEB:

TWISTED

May 2019

OBSESSED

July 2019

BOUND

August 2019

WEB OF DESIRE:

SPARK

Jan. 14, 2020

FLAME

February 25, 2020

ASHES

April 7, 2020

DANGEROUS WEB:

Prequel: "Danger's First Kiss"

DUSK

November 2020

DARK

January 2021

DAWN

February 2021

* * *

THE INFIDELITY SERIES:

BETRAYAL

Book #1

October 2015

CUNNING

Book #2

January 2016

DECEPTION

Book #3

May 2016

ENTRAPMENT

Book #4

September 2016

FIDELITY

Book #5

January 2017

* * *

THE CONSEQUENCES SERIES:

CONSEQUENCES

(Book #1)

August 2011

TRUTH

(Book #2)

October 2012

CONVICTED

(Book #3)

October 2013

REVEALED

(Book #4)

Previously titled: Behind His Eyes Convicted: The Missing Years

June 2014

BEYOND THE CONSEQUENCES

(Book #5)

January 2015

RIPPLES (Consequences stand-alone)

October 2017

CONSEQUENCES COMPANION READS:

BEHIND HIS EYES-CONSEQUENCES

January 2014

BEHIND HIS EYES-TRUTH

March 2014

* * *

STAND ALONE MAFIA THRILLER:

PRICE OF HONOR

Available Now

* * *

STAND-ALONE ROMANTIC THRILLER:

ON THE EDGE

May 2022

***

THE LIGHT DUET:

Published through Thomas and Mercer Amazon exclusive

INTO THE LIGHT

June 2016

AWAY FROM THE DARK

October 2016

* * *

TALES FROM THE DARK SIDE SERIES:

INSIDIOUS

(All books in this series are stand-alone erotic thrillers)

Released October 2014

* * *

ALEATHA'S LIGHTER ONES:

PLUS ONE

Stand-alone fun, sexy romance

May 2017

ANOTHER ONE

Stand-alone fun, sexy romance

May 2018

ONE NIGHT

Stand-alone, sexy contemporary romance

September 2017

A SECRET ONE

April 2018

MY ALWAYS ONE

Stand-Alone, sexy friends to lovers contemporary romance

July 2021

QUINTESSENTIALLY THE ONE

Stand-alone, small-town, second-chance, secret baby contemporary romance

July 2022

MY ONLY ONE

Stand-alone, small-town, best friend's sister,

grump/sunshine contemporary romance.

July 2023

* * *

INDULGENCE SERIES:

UNEXPECTED

August 2018

UNCONVENTIONAL

January 2018

UNFORGETTABLE

October 2019

UNDENIABLE

August 2020

About the Author

Aleatha Romig is a New York Times, Wall Street Journal, and USA Today bestselling author who lives in Indiana, USA. She has raised three children with her high school sweetheart and husband of over thirty years. Before she became a full-time author, she worked days as a dental hygienist and spent her nights writing. Now, when she's not imagining mind-blowing twists and turns, she likes to spend her time with her family and friends. Her other pastimes include reading and creating heroes/anti-heroes who haunt your dreams!

Aleatha impresses with her versatility in writing. She released her first novel, CONSEQUENCES, in August of 2011. CONSEQUENCES, a dark romance, became a bestselling series with five novels and two companions released from 2011 through 2015. The compelling and epic story of Anthony and Claire Rawlings has graced more than half a million e-readers. Her first stand-alone smart, sexy thriller

INSIDIOUS was next. Then Aleatha released the five-novel INFIDELITY series, a romantic suspense saga, that took the reading world by storm, the final book landing on three of the top bestseller lists. She ventured into traditional publishing with Thomas and Mercer. Her books INTO THE LIGHT and AWAY FROM THE DARK were published through this mystery/thriller publisher in 2016. In the spring of 2017, Aleatha again ventured into a different genre with her first fun and sexy stand-alone romantic comedy with the USA Today bestseller PLUS ONE. She continued with ONE NIGHT and ANOTHER ONE. If you like fun, sexy, novellas that make your heart pound, try her UNCONVENTIONAL and UNEXPECTED. In 2018 Aleatha returned to her dark romance roots with SPARROW WEBS.

Aleatha is a "Published Author's Network" member of the Romance Writers of America and PEN America. She is represented by Kevan Lyon of Marsal Lyon Literary Agency and Dani Sanchez with Wildfire Marketing.

facebook.com/aleatharomig

twitter.com/aleatharomig

instagram.com/aleatharomig